MOUNTAIN SHADOWS

When Jenna Manning's mother dies, she makes a series of shocking discoveries. She learns that her mother had cut her out of her will . . . but then finds that, along with the thriller writer Luke Grantley, she's part-owner of the family's old home in Cumbria. Jenna decides to visit 'Brackwith' and finds the injured Luke in residence. But it's only after stumbling upon the truth about her father, that Jenna and Luke realise their lives have become completely entwined.

Books by Paula Williams
in the Linford Romance Library:

PLACE OF HEALING
FINDING ANNABEL

PAULA WILLIAMS

MOUNTAIN SHADOWS

Complete and Unabridged

LINFORD
Leicester

First published in Great Britain in 2011

First Linford Edition
published 2012

British Library CIP Data

Williams, Paula.
   Mountain shadows.- -
   (Linford romance library)
   1. Love stories.
   2. Large type books.
   I. Title II. Series
   823.9'2–dc23

   ISBN 978–1–4448–1327–2

Published by
F. A. Thorpe (Publishing)
Anstey, Leicestershire

Set by Words & Graphics Ltd.
Anstey, Leicestershire
Printed and bound in Great Britain by
T. J. International Ltd., Padstow, Cornwall

This book is printed on acid-free paper

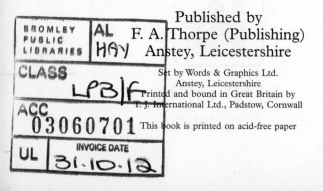

1

Manning, Lynda Joan, beloved mother of James and Jenna, died peacefully at her home on January 6 after a long illness bravely borne. Funeral to be held at 2pm, January 12 at St John's Church, Chedcombe, Somerset. No flowers, please, but donations may be sent to Cancer Relief Macmillan Fund.

Jenna Manning was, as always, in perfect control as she followed her mother's coffin into the churchyard. The other mourners pulled their coats tighter against the cruel wind that danced in and out of the yew trees. But not Jenna. At her side, her brother James hunched his shoulders against the wind but Jenna walked straight and tall, her short copper curls a flame of colour against her black clothes.

Yet, out of sight of sympathetic eyes, her hands were clenched so tightly by her side that her knuckles showed white and her nails left tiny, crescent-shaped imprints on her palms. But you'd have to know Jenna well to notice these signs. And few people did.

As they filed towards the open grave, Jenna looked at those who'd braved the bitter afternoon to come and noted, with grim satisfaction, who had not. He'd phoned three days ago to say that he would like to attend and at first, she'd thought he was a friend of her mother's.

'I'd be grateful if you and your brother could spare me a few minutes after the funeral,' he went on. 'There's something I need to discuss with you both. I realise it's a bad time but it won't take long, I promise.'

'How did you say you knew my mother, Mr . . . ?' There was something about the way he spoke, an edge to his voice that made Jenna anxious to place

2

him. 'I'm sorry, I didn't catch your name,' she prompted.

'I didn't give it,' he said. 'But it's Grantley. Luke Grantley. I was a friend of your father's and I — '

Jenna pushed the memory away as the small procession halted at the open grave. James moved closer to her but Jenna stepped away from him and stood alone as the coffin was lowered into the ground. Only when clods of earth rattled down on the polished lid did she show any sign of emotion. She stretched out a hand, fingers splayed, as if in an attempt to protect her mother from the falling earth.

Jenna looked down on the coffin. Several times during the last weeks of her life, her mother had started to talk about something that had been 'troubling her'. But each time she stopped, saying she'd tell her later. And now Jenna would never know, and the finality of the thought saddened her.

Yet she could shed no tears. She never cried — or hadn't done so for a long time. She threw a red rose, her mother's favourite flower, on to the coffin, where it bounced once, rolled over and settled among the clods of dirt.

★　★　★

'And I leave the property known as Robin's Cottage, Lower Lane, Chedcombe, Somerset to my son, James, in its entirety, the contents of that property to be shared between him and my daughter, Jenna, as they see fit.'

Jenna made no attempt to make any sense of the words that ricocheted around inside her head. Instead she concentrated on a shaft of sunlight that pierced the heavy January clouds, illuminating the smooth, pink skin on the top of Mr Bennington's head. She avoided his eyes, for she'd already seen his embarrassed flicker of sympathy. And she didn't want his, or anybody else's, sympathy.

Her long, slender fingers lay quite

still in her lap, giving a misleading impression of calm. From her mid-teens she'd developed an ability to hide her true feelings and was never more thankful for it than now, when her safe, familiar world had been turned upside down.

This, then, she supposed, was what her mother had been trying to tell her in the few days before she'd died. That she'd cut her out of her will, leaving their home to James and nothing to her. She shook her head, still unable to take it in. Why? Why had she done it? Did James know?

Yet James looked as stunned as she felt. She straightened her back and took a deep, steadying breath.

'Jenna?' Edward Bennington sounded concerned. 'It's been a shock, my dear. Would you like me to go through it again?'

Jenna nodded, her hands now white-knuckled in her lap. She didn't need to hear the words again but it bought her a little more time to compose herself.

'As I said, it appears your mother was anxious to redress what she felt was an injustice done to your brother under the terms of your father's will.'

'Dad's will?' Jenna stared at James, who looked as mystified as she felt.

He shook his head. 'But we didn't know Dad had made a will,' he said. 'Or, rather, I suppose he must have done but we never knew anything about it. That was seven years ago. We were only in our teens. Presumably, Mum dealt with all that.'

The elderly solicitor shuffled in his seat and straightened the already neatly-stacked files on his desk. 'Quite.' He cleared his throat. 'I advised your dear mother many times to make this known to you but she . . . well, let's say she preferred to do things in her own time.'

'Which just ran out,' James said in a harsh voice.

'Of course I didn't act for your father,' Edward Bennington went on. 'So, legally speaking, I know nothing of the contents of his will — only what your mother chose to tell me as a friend.'

For Heaven's sake, get on with it! Jenna wanted to scream but instead, in a voice so calm she surprised even herself, she asked, 'Which was?'

'Your father left something in trust for you, Jenna, until you were . . . ah . . . twenty-one.'

'Twenty-one?' James said it before Jenna could. 'But she was twenty-one over two years ago. How come we didn't know about it until now? Why didn't Mum tell Jenna about it then — and me, come to that?'

Edward Bennington shook his head. 'Had I been aware of the situation, I'd have urged your mother most strongly to tell you both, but I'd no idea, no idea at all until I visited her a couple of weeks ago. No doubt you recall the occasion, Jenna?'

Jenna nodded. She did indeed. Her mother had been tearful and agitated before the solicitor's visit but calmer after he'd left. The two had been friends for years and Jenna had put the improvement in her mother's spirits down to the reassurance of seeing her old confidant. She'd had no idea that Mr Bennington's visit was a professional one.

'I told her the least she could do at this late stage was to tell you as soon as possible,' he said. 'But she got so upset I became alarmed, in view of . . . of the advanced stage of her illness. So, to spare her further distress I suggested she wrote a letter of explanation which I would give to you at . . . at the appropriate time.'

He re-straightened the same stack of files, then pulled out a letter from a drawer and handed it to Jenna. Her mother's small, neat handwriting leapt at her.

My dear Jenna,
Edward suggested I write this. He says you'll probably be upset, maybe even angry when you read it. But

8

please don't be. Don't be cross with James, either, for he knows nothing about this.

I tried to tell you several times, but somehow couldn't find the right words. I was a coward, I know, but we've been getting on so well lately and I didn't want to spoil it.

Jenna sighed, ran a distracted hand through her short springy curls and read on.

You remember Brackwith, I'm sure — how upset you were when we left? Well, when your father died, he left it to you in his will. I must say, it came as a shock to me, as I thought he'd got rid of the place when he sold our house in Manchester. I didn't tell you at the time. You were so ill after he died, remember? I was worried that it might make you worse.

Jenna had to stop reading to regain control of her trembling hands and to try and make sense of what she'd read. She owned Brackwith! It had been there, waiting for her, all the time. If only she'd known. If only . . .

Anyway, to tell the truth, I'd more or less forgotten about it until a few months back when I had a letter from a solicitor in Kendal, on behalf of a client with an offer on the place. He obviously thought I was the owner. And the amount he offered! It's only a run-down collection of farm buildings after all, no hot water, no electricity (how I hated the place!) yet he offered twice as much as my little cottage here is worth. His client wants to turn the place into one of those fancy hotels or something.

Well, it struck me how unfair this was on James. Your father always did have a down on him, you know. Maybe because James is so much like me. Your father could be a difficult man, Jenna. Never forget that.

No chance of that, Jenna thought. Ever since her parents' divorce thirteen years ago she'd never been allowed to forget what a 'difficult' man he was. She bit her bottom lip hard at the thought of her mother still ensuring she got that particular message from beyond the grave.

That's why I've left the cottage to James. Of course if you want to live there, you can. I'm sure Edward can arrange for you to buy it from James once you've sold Brackwith. He's written to the Kendal solicitor, telling him to get in touch with you although I've asked him to delay things if he can, for my sake.

You've been good to me these past few months. I don't find this sort of thing easy but I want you to know I appreciate it.

Be happy, Jenna. Look out for James. He's going to need a lot of support if he's to fulfil his great potential. Make sure he does. He's made me so very proud. And so, too, of course, have you.

With love, Mum.

Jenna read the letter a second time. Did it really mean she owned Brackwith? For the moment, nothing else mattered beyond that amazing fact. All these years, when she'd imagined strangers living there, it had been there, waiting for her. Her father had kept his promise after all.

She passed the letter to James who read it quickly.

'You're going to sell it, of course, Jen,' he said. 'After all, you don't want to saddle yourself with a load of run-down buildings, do you?'

Edward Bennington cleared his throat. 'There are — ' he began, straightening the files once more. 'Ah ... certain conditions regarding the property that your mother didn't, er, didn't go into in her letter.'

'Conditions?' Jenna's heart sank. Had her mother got things wrong? Was the

12

place the subject of a compulsory purchase order? Or, worse still, had its condition deteriorated so much, a demolition order? 'What conditions?'

'Your mother didn't tell you the full story,' he said, his eyes troubled. 'You don't own the property outright, I'm afraid. There's a co-owner I'm afraid, and a condition stating that neither can sell their share in the property without first offering it to the other party.'

'This other party — ' Jenna began.

'Is the client of the Kendal solicitor your mother refers to, who wishes to purchase your interest in the property. I have to say he's made an extremely generous offer — one I strongly recommend you accept.'

Her chair made an ugly scraping sound as she got up and turned towards the window. With unseeing eyes she stared at the traffic in the street below, building up towards the rush hour. She felt like a child given a longed-for ice cream, only to have it snatched away before she could take even one small bite.

From far away, she heard James ask, 'Who is he — this 'other party', as you call him?'

'Your mother didn't explain the connection between him and your late father and I'm afraid I don't know much about him. Except, that is, for his name.' He searched with maddening slowness among his papers. 'Ah, here we are. His name is Grantley. A Mr Luke Grantley. Does that mean anything to you?'

Jenna whirled round, her eyes blazing deep emerald against her white face.

James looked puzzled. 'Not *the* Luke Grantley, I suppose? The thriller writer?'

'The very same,' Jenna snapped, then turned back to the window as she struggled for self-control.

'But what's his connection with us? With Dad?'

'With us, none. With Dad, he was — ' she stopped and forced herself to regain control. This was neither the time nor the place. 'He did a lot of climbing with Dad at one time.'

'As I said, Jenna,' Edward Bennington went on, 'Mr Grantley's offer is a generous one and in view of the fact you don't own the property outright and your — ' He pushed his hand through his non-existent hair. 'Your situation — I strongly advise you to accept it. You're scarcely in a secure enough financial position to buy him out, so if — '

'Thank you, Mr Bennington.' Jenna stood up. She had to get out of the stuffy room, away from his well-meaning sympathy, as soon as possible. 'You've been very kind. But if you'll excuse us, I'd like to get out of town before the traffic gets too bad.'

'Keep in touch then, my dear,' he said. 'And promise me that you'll think about Mr Grantley's offer.'

Think about it? She thought of the brief, bitter telephone conversation she'd had with him the day before her mother's funeral. She thought, too, of

15

the long, resentful years she'd spent hating him, wishing he'd died on that faraway mountain instead of her father.

'Oh yes, Mr Bennington,' she said, her voice icy as she regained her composure. 'I'll think about Mr Grantley's offer. I can promise you that.'

2

'Jenna, you're not serious!' James exclaimed, when she'd phoned him to tell him of her plans.

'I've never been more serious in my life. I want to get this whole business of Brackwith sorted out and the best, the quickest way is to go up there and get on with it — and there's no time like the present.'

'But you can't drive all the way there today. It'll take you hours and the forecast is lousy again, especially for the north. Why not wait, at least until the weekend and we'll go up together? Oh no — I can't. I've got a concert Saturday night.'

James was a talented musician and, in his third year at the Royal College of Music, was already carving out a promising career for himself.

'Maybe you could get that guy

Steven, who kept ringing you, to take you. He sounded keen.'

'I wouldn't dream of asking Steven. Besides, I want to see that Kendal solicitor and I don't imagine he works at weekends. It's been a fortnight since we saw Mr Bennington and I want to get things sorted without any more delay.' She sighed. 'Besides, I fancy a few days in the Lake District. I've booked into a hotel in Ambleside. The one right in the main street. Remember it?'

'All I remember about the area around Brackwith was that it was like Siberia, whatever the season,' James said with a shiver at the memory. 'Why go there now?'

'Because it's so beautiful even at this time of the year and I need a break. Looking after Mum was exhausting, you know, especially the last week.'

There was a long, uncomfortable pause and Jenna could just imagine him raking his fingers through his thick; blond hair.

'Yeah, I know,' he mumbled when it became obvious Jenna wasn't going to break the silence. 'Look, I'm truly sorry about that, Jen. I should've come when you sent for me, I know, but I couldn't face it. I'd rather remember her as she was.'

So would I! Jenna wanted to scream down the phone at him. *I'd have liked to have walked away from her and her illness saying I couldn't cope, too, but if I had, she'd have died alone and frightened in hospital instead of with peace and dignity in her own bed.*

But the angry words died on her lips. What was the point? It wouldn't change anything, not now.

She muttered something soothing, ended the call, then threw her already packed weekend bag into the car and began the long drive north.

* * *

The weather was every bit as atrocious as James had predicted. Rain hit the

19

windscreen with the rattle of distant machine-gun fire. The sky was so low and heavy with cloud, the motorway so thick with spray, that in the distance — or so it seemed to Jenna's tired eyes — road and sky merged into a single large grey cloud that engulfed an endless stream of red tail-lights.

It was after four o'clock and beginning to get dark when she reached Ambleside. But the hotel was bright and cheerful, with a welcoming log fire burning in the grate. She was delighted with her cosy, low-ceilinged bedroom, and the comfortable bed looked very inviting. But she resisted, worried that if she lay down and closed her eyes, she might sleep for a week.

Instead, she relaxed into a chair by the window, leaned back against the deep, cushioned back and let the tension of the long drive melt away. The window faced one of the fells that cradled Ambleside. She looked up to its top, white-capped from earlier snow-falls and for a moment experienced a longing to be up there, to feel the icy wind sting her face, to look down on the toy-town houses below.

She'd done exactly that once, with her father beside her, gasping with delight at the spectacular scenery, proud of having kept pace with him up the steep, rocky climb. Not for them the easy route taken by tourists out for an afternoon stroll. He was, after all, John Manning, the well-known mountaineer, and she was his daughter who would one day become an equally famous mountaineer.

What plans they'd made that day. What dreams they'd dreamed up there, where he looked on with pleasure as Jenna fell in love with high places, with climbing itself. It had been so easy, the falling in love. But then so hard, the pain of falling out of love that followed.

She drew the heavy curtains, shutting out the view of the fells, now faintly menacing, looming shadows in the fading light.

She shivered. She'd been mad to

come. There was nothing here for her any more; not even Brackwith. Especially not Brackwith. If she felt threatened by the hills around Ambleside, how much worse would she feel about the harsher landscape around Brackwith? How would she feel, looking up and seeing the stark, grey outlines of Brackwith Pike itself?

Tomorrow, she decided, she'd make contact with the Kendal solicitor and Luke Grantley could then do what he liked with the place. There was no point in holding on to the past. It wouldn't change anything. Yes, that's what she would do. She'd take the money he was offering and then she'd never have to see the place again.

And yet, the next day, it was as if she was on some sort of automatic pilot. Instead of taking the main road back towards Kendal, she found herself on the road that led through the narrow valley towards Brackwith. It was little more than a country lane, with high stone walls either side and few passing places. She didn't remember it being quite so narrow.

No harm in going along as far as the turning. Seeing the place for one last time, she reasoned. *I may as well see what I'm signing away — help me to find some closure.*

She stopped to consult her map. She knew the farmhouse and buildings lay at the end of a long, winding track and hoped she'd recognise the turning after so many years. She hoped, too, that the unmade, stone-strewn farm track hadn't deteriorated too much in that time.

To her surprise, she found it easily. *Might as well drive up to the bend to get a view of the house,* she thought.

Slowly she eased the car along the track, stones scrunching under her wheels as she did so. A few Herdwick sheep — a breed local to the Lake District with grey coats and pretty white faces — looked up, briefly anxious, then went back to cropping the sparse winter grass.

She drove carefully around a sharp corner where the track fell away to one side and stopped. With her hands gripping the steering wheel tightly, she stared at the sight of Brackwith Farm House some five hundred yards ahead, a huddle of stone buildings nestling at the foot of the dramatic grey cliffs that led up to Brackwith Pike itself.

★ ★ ★

Nothing had changed. It was all exactly the same as the day she'd left. She'd stopped close to the spot where her mother had waited with James in the car, impatient to be gone, while eleven-year-old Jenna had spun out her goodbyes for as long as she could.

'Goodbye, chickens. Goodbye, sheep. Goodbye, river — '

The car horn tooted crossly. Jenna turned to her father, eyes filled with panic.

'Why won't you come, Dad?' she asked him for what must have been the

24

tenth time that morning. 'Why?'

'You know why,' he answered, his face as white as hers, his mouth set in a hard line. 'We've been through all that. But we'll see each other soon and you can come back any time you want. You know that.'

'I'll never come back,' she cried and clung to him, his jacket rough against her wet cheeks. 'I'll never see the chickens again, or the sheep, or the river. I know it. I'll never come back.'

He held her away from him and looked deep into her tear-filled eyes.

'Look at me, Jenna,' His voice was quiet but urgent. 'Listen to what I'm saying, because I promise it's the truth. You will come back to Brackwith. If you want to, you'll be back. And the chickens, the sheep, the river and me — we'll all be here waiting for you. I promise. Now, go with your mother and be a good girl for her. But never forget that Brackwith will always be here waiting for you and so will I. You have my solemn promise on that.'

★ ★ ★

Suddenly Jenna became aware of pain in her fingers. She'd been gripping the steering wheel so tightly that her hands had stiffened with cramp. She rubbed them to restore the circulation, staring ahead as if she expected to see her father striding towards her, red hair blown wild in the driving wind.

He'd kept his promise after all.

Now, she was going to make a promise to him. Her mother's letter had mentioned how Luke Grantley wanted to turn Brackwith into a hotel, something her father would have hated.

'He's not going to do it, Dad,' she murmured. 'This place meant so much to you. No way am I going to let him turn it into some fancy hotel, full of braying tourists tearing about in their four-wheel drives. It's not going to happen. I promise.'

She released the brake and the car rolled gently down the slope towards the house. As she did so, the first flakes

26

of snow began to fall. The waiter who had served her breakfast had been right after all. He'd predicted that there was more snow on the way today.

By the time she'd parked, the snow was falling heavily, reducing visibility to a few yards in any direction, blotting out not only Brackwith Pike, but the track she'd just driven on.

Over the past eleven years, she'd become accustomed to the less severe winters of the West Country, and the speed and severity of the storm's onset took her by surprise. She was almost blown over by the force of the wind as she stepped out of the car. She pulled her coat closer and ran across the yard to the front door, cursing herself for not having the key Mr Bennington had given her, ready in her hand.

It took several uncomfortable minutes, with the wind lashing snow in her face and tugging at her clothes, before she found the key deep in the bottom of her bag. With fingers that trembled from anxiety and excitement as well as cold, she turned the key and let herself in.

The place hadn't changed. It was the same wide hallway, the same flagstone floor and the same set of black and white photographs of mountains down one side. The same grandfather clock stood in the corner and as she stood there remembering, it drew the same familiar wheezy breath before striking three o'clock.

Everything was the same, yet different. For a while she couldn't work out what it was until she realised: she no longer had to stand on tiptoe to look at the photographs.

To her right was the door to her father's study. She went in, seeing the sagging armchair still piled with the same shabby cushions she used to burrow into as she watched him work. Her gaze swept the clock, the book-cases, even the ice axe he used as a door wedge. His desk, littered with books and papers, looked as if he'd just gone into the next room for something.

She looked towards the door that led to the small room he used as a bedroom when he worked late into the night and didn't want to disturb the family. She approached it — and froze. From the other side came a cough. A small, quiet sound she might not have heard if she'd not been half expecting it.

I'll be waiting for you, I promise, he'd said.

'Dad?'

She knew it couldn't be him. He'd been dead for seven years and she didn't believe in ghosts. Yet she sensed his presence so strongly; she felt she only had to take one last step and she'd surely be face to face with him.

She hesitated, hand on the doorknob. What would she say? What could she say? *I'm sorry? Forgive me?* Trite, inadequate words, yet words that needed to be said. She'd know no peace until they were and it was here, surely, she'd find that peace.

If, that is, she had the courage.

She opened the door.

As she did so, the man in the bed sat up. It took several confused seconds to register the fact that his hair was not the wild rust-coloured mop that had been her father's, but smooth and black as a raven's wing. His eyes were not the green that mirrored her own but a strange light blue — so bright, so piercing and so unexpected in that dark complexion that they looked like blue-tinged icicles. He stared at her, black eyebrows arched in surprise at her entrance.

The face was indeed familiar. But it was not, of course, her father's. It was the man whom she hated most in the whole world. The last one she wanted to see.

'So you got here after all,' Luke Grantley said. 'I must say, I was beginning to wonder whether you'd make it.'

3

Jenna had always thought that the phrase 'too shocked to move' was a meaningless cliché. Now she knew better as she stood, one hand on the door handle, shocked, frozen. Her brain felt gripped by the same paralysis as she struggled to make sense of the scene in front of her. Luke Grantley, for Heaven's sake. In her father's bed. Was she dreaming? Hallucinating? A nightmare, surely?

'I thought the weather would have put you off,' he said. 'It's getting grim out there, isn't it?'

'It's starting to snow — ' Jenna began, then stopped and shook her head. What was she doing? So many times she'd imagined meeting Luke Grantley, going over in her mind the things she'd say. She had, she thought, rehearsed every possible scenario. Except this one.

She had never, even in her most outrageous fantasies, imagined that their first exchange would be mundane chit-chat about the weather.

'Sister Martin said she'd found someone to come up and 'do' for me as she so quaintly put it,' he said. 'But I didn't think you'd come when I heard the forecast. If they say it's going to snow around here, it snows. Have you come far?'

Cleaning? Come far? She forced her shocked brain into action, as he waited for her reply. He hadn't recognised her.

No reason why he should, of course. She'd have known his face anywhere, for she'd followed his increasingly successful career as a thriller writer over the past seven years with a bitter curiosity. And yet, he'd mistaken her for his cleaning lady.

'Ambleside,' she answered, which was a sort of truth. 'I've only come from Ambleside. Not far.'

'Did you bring the shopping?'

She stared at him. 'I'm sorry? I'm

afraid I don't — '

'Sister Martin said that you'd bring up some bits and pieces I need.'

'Oh. I didn't know. It was all such a rush. I've got some things in the car, though.'

'Well, I certainly don't need a nurse, if that was what you thought you were here for!'

She looked up startled by his sharpness. 'Look, I'm sorry.' She backed towards the door. 'There's been a mistake — '

'Give me strength!' A lock of his hair dropped in front of his eyes, as James's often did. Unlike James, though, he made no attempt to flick it back. 'There's really no need to run away,' he snapped. 'I'm hardly likely to chase you around the bedroom, am I?'

She followed his eyes and saw what he'd intended her to see. She gasped, her hand to her mouth. How could she have been so blind? How could she have missed the wheelchair by the side of the bed?

'Well?' he went on. 'Didn't they tell you about the wheelchair? Does it make a difference?'

Jenna shook her head. 'Of course it doesn't. It's just — I didn't know,' she whispered. 'Did you have . . . ? I'm sorry. I shouldn't ask. I didn't mean . . . '

'What you mean is, did I have an accident or is it a permanent disability?' His voice was harsh, his eyes cold but steady as he answered the questions she hadn't been able to put into words. 'The answer to both is yes. Yes, I had an accident and yes, it's likely to be permanent.'

His words hung in the air between them. Jenna's heart was banging so hard against her ribcage, she thought he must hear it. For seven years, she'd hated this man and wished he'd died instead of her father. For seven years, she'd imagined what she'd say to him, what she'd do to him, how she'd hurt him.

But she'd never imagined the empty wheelchair, waiting for him by the side of his bed.

After what seemed hours but could only have been seconds, she gradually became aware of the storm outside. It was working itself to a frenzy, as it shook the windows and caused the lights to flicker.

'I'm sorry.' Luke smiled, a rueful, apologetic smile that softened his face and made him look much younger. 'I shouldn't have shouted. That was unforgivably rude. I'm a selfish, arrogant, self-pitying bastard. Go on. Say it.'

Jenna met his gaze. 'All right,' she returned after a long pause as she struggled to regain control. 'You're a selfish, arrogant bastard.'

Their eyes held, hers daring him to erupt into anger, his surprised and wary. Outside, the wind howled as it funnelled between buildings, hurling snow into strange, sculpted shapes. But inside, the only sound was the ticking of the small clock on his bedside table.

'You forgot self-pitying,' he said challengingly, the first to break the silence.

She shrugged but said nothing.

Then he laughed and the wary look in his eyes disappeared. 'Okay, I asked for that,' he said. 'Let's start again, shall we? What did you say your name was?'

'I didn't. But it's J — ' She stopped herself in time. 'It's Jane. Jane Bennington.'

She didn't think Mr Bennington would mind. It was the best she could come up with at short notice.

'So, have I frightened you off, Jane Bennington, or are you going to give me a chance to show I'm not the monster you obviously believe I am?'

'What do you mean?' she asked, her throat tightening. Did he know who she was, after all? Had she given herself away already?

'You looked as if you were trying to work out how long it would take you to reach the front door,' he said. 'But I wouldn't worry on that score, Jane. You'd beat me by a mile.'

Jenna forced a smile, which she hoped looked more relaxed than she felt. 'Quite possibly,' she said. Her smile faded as she went on, 'Do you mind talking about your accident?'

He shrugged then shook his head. 'I've talked about little else since it happened.'

'When was that?'

'A couple of weeks ago.' The light, bright blue of his eyes had changed to the brooding grey of an approaching storm. 'A climbing accident. I fell off a mountain, that mountain out there to be precise.' He gestured towards Brackwith Pike. 'A genuine accident. No one to blame, except of course, myself, for a moment's carelessness.'

A cold hand of remembered fear and grief clutched at Jenna's heart. 'There's no such thing as a genuine climbing accident,' she said, unable to stop herself quoting her mother's often-repeated words. 'There's always someone to blame.'

A snatch of a poem she'd learned as a child to impress her father returned to taunt her, as it had done many times before.

The shadow of the high mountain is a long one indeed, it began. *It casts over hill, over dale —*

She couldn't — she wouldn't — remember any more. She shivered and turned away from him. The high mountain had certainly cast a shadow over her life, over her parents' lives . . . and now over Luke's.

It didn't matter that the accidents happened on different mountains. Their shadows were just as long, just as deep.

He was watching her, an unfathomable expression in those strange eyes. 'Are you speaking from personal experience, Jane?' he asked, his voice soft, his eyes fixed on hers.

She flushed, realising how close she'd come once again to giving herself away. She wasn't cut out for deception. Maybe it would be better if she stopped it now, told him the truth, signed her share in Brackwith over to him and —

He was living here! Why hadn't that occurred to her before? She looked around the small bedroom, seeing it properly for the first time. Why hadn't she noticed the modern furniture, the curtains, the carpets? She'd been expecting the place to be empty, except of course for her father's ghost, when all the time Luke Grantley had been living here, in the house that was half hers. There was something going on, and she intended to find out what. And until she did, she was going to play along with the misunderstanding.

'I'm sorry.' She pretended a coolness she didn't feel. 'You asked if I was speaking from experience. I got lost on top of the fells once when I was little. I wasn't hurt, just frightened, but it's left me . . . well, let's say I don't like mountains.'

And that was as near the truth as she dared to venture.

'That's a pity,' he said, looking at her in such a way that it was impossible for her to turn away. 'Sometimes, you know, Jane, the best way to deal with fear is to face it head-on. Often you find then that the thing you feared is nothing like as frightening as the fear itself.'

She broke free of his hypnotic gaze and noticed for the first time the angry-looking bruise along his right cheekbone. She noticed, too, the fan of tiny white lines by the corners of his eyes, the same marks her father used to have, caused by screwing up his eyes in the sunlight.

When she was little, she used to love tracing her fingers along her father's white lines and for one crazy moment, she almost reached out one gentle, very cool finger to trace those fine lines around Luke Grantley's eyes, to soothe the pain from his cheekbone and to push back the lock of hair that had fallen over one eye.

Had she gone mad? Stark, staring mad? She-stuffed her hand deep into her pocket, as if afraid it might act out that crazy impulse of its own volition. What was she doing? This was Luke Grantley, for Heaven's sake, the man who'd stolen her father from her, then left him to die alone on a mountain.

Yesterday's journey must have affected her more than she realised. Tiredness engulfed her. She'd had enough. She just wanted to get away, as far and as fast as possible.

As she turned to go, a vicious wind blasted the side of the house, flinging wedges of snow against the window panes, where they slid down in short, angry hisses. Again, the lights dimmed, went out and then came back on again.

'If you don't go soon,' Luke remarked, 'you could be here for days. I don't like the way the wind's changed direction. That often means bad news. Two, or was it three winters ago, I was holed up here for three weeks. Nobody could get in and I couldn't get out.'

What? Her exhaustion vanished as she realised the significance of what he'd said. Two or three winters ago? 'How long have you lived here?' she asked.

'Three or four years now, off and on,' he said. 'Although I first came here briefly when I was fourteen. That visit changed my life and that's no exaggeration. I suppose it's been my spiritual home ever since. The only place in the world where I ever feel truly at home — and where I always come back to if things go wrong.'

Jenna looked at the wheelchair. *Things have gone tragically wrong for him this time*, she thought and for the first time since her father's death, it occurred to her that maybe there were, after all, worse things than dying in a climbing accident. Maybe there were times when it was worse not to die.

Then the old bitterness returned and she dismissed the thought. Luke Grantley had a chance, however slight, of recovery. Her father had none.

'How lucky for you then,' she said, her voice cold, 'to be able to buy the place that meant so much to you. I imagine places like this don't come on the market often.'

If she hadn't been looking for the pause, she wouldn't have noticed it, for

42

it was the briefest hesitation, over in the flicker of an eyelid. But it had been there all the same.

'I didn't buy it,' he said. 'It was left to me.'

Once again, the lights in the house flickered.

'If you don't go soon,' he went on, his calm voice a marked contrast to the storm and yet, Jenna fancied, just as menacing, 'the track will become impassable.'

She crossed to the window and peered out, straining to see her car in the snow-covered yard. Her heart sank.

'Actually I think it's already too late,' she said.

He gave an exclamation of annoyance. 'Well, in that case the best thing to do is to wait for the storm to blow itself out, and then go out and see what it's like. Sometimes, you find it's a lot of noise and loose snow, with nothing much to show for it. You really shouldn't have come, though, you know.'

He leaned back against the pillows, as if exhausted by the effort of making conversation. She saw a deep frown crease his forehead and beads of sweat appear.

'Are you in pain? Can I get you something?' She was alarmed at the way the colour had suddenly drained from his face. 'Shall I call the nurse — or a doctor?'

He shook his head. 'It'll pass,' he said, through tightly clenched jaws. He stretched towards a bottle of pills on the bedside table. Jenna reached it before him, read the label, took out a couple of pills and passed them to him with a glass of water. He leaned back, eyes closed and Jenna could see the spasm was gradually loosening its grip.

She leaned across and, in an instinctive gesture born from the experience of nursing her mother, smoothed the sheets and straightened his pillow. She laid a cool hand on his brow, thankful to feel that his temperature was normal. Then, unable to resist it, she smoothed back his hair from his face.

At once, his eyes opened, clear, blue and almost pain-free. 'Well, now, if you aren't the bargain of the century?' He grinned up at her. 'A cleaning lady with healing hands.'

'The spasm has passed, I take it?' she said, conscious of the slow flush burning her cheeks and hoping he hadn't noticed.

'In record time,' he said. 'You'd better stay around, in case I have another.'

'I — well, I think you're right about the storm,' she said, turning her scarlet cheeks away from him. 'Best to wait it out. As you say, it may well have blown itself out in an hour. In the meantime, I'll make myself useful. Would you like some tea?'

He was laughing at her discomfort, at her blushes. The thought made her cheeks burn even more. She had to get out of this room and do something, anything.

'I'd prefer you brushed my fevered brow again, but failing that, tea would be fine,' he said.

She turned towards the door and was half way across the study when she heard him call out. There was no laughter in his voice now. He called again, his voice louder, angrier.

'Jane, damn you! Come back here at once.'

4

Jenna froze, alarmed by the anger in his voice. Had he worked out who she was after all?

'What's wrong?' she asked, turning back, sounding a lot calmer than she felt.

'You don't need to go through my study. You can reach the kitchen from that door to your right which opens directly into the hall. I was — am — working on a draft of my next book that's at a critical stage. I'd hate it to be disturbed.'

She turned to him with what she hoped was an expression of calm reproach on her face. 'You only had to ask,' she said.

'You're right, of course,' he said with a sudden disarming smile. 'I'm sorry I barked at you like that. I'm being a selfish, arrogant bastard again, aren't I?'

She didn't return his smile but nodded and left through the door he'd indicated. Not that she needed directions, of course. The old farmhouse was still as familiar to her as her mother's Somerset cottage. Except that now, of course, it was James's cottage — or would be for as long as it took the estate agent to sell it. Unlike her, James had lost no time in taking steps to turn his inheritance into hard cash.

Although, to be fair to him, he had done so only after she'd convinced him that she didn't want to stay on at the cottage. When her mother became ill, she'd taken indefinite leave from her job in Bristol and found a work colleague to take over the rental of her flat. But as soon as she'd got things at Brackwith sorted, she'd have to find a job and flat, maybe back in Bristol. Or even London.

The kitchen was a big surprise. At first glance the only thing familiar about it was the window, which looked across what used to be the collecting yard for the cattle back when it was a working farm, to the valley beyond. Not that she could see very much of the view now through the lashing snow-storm, just the vague outlines of a series of snow-covered objects — one of which, she realised with dismay, must be her own car.

Luke had been right. There was no way she was going anywhere at the moment. She glanced anxiously at her watch. It was nearly four o'clock. Even if the snow stopped now, it would soon be too dark to drive along that uneven track with its adverse cambers and crumbling edges.

Whatever the dangers of staying with Luke — and they could be minimised if she kept a clear head — they were preferable to crashing into a snowdrift, or worse.

She looked around the refurbished kitchen and smiled. How her mother had hated Brackwith with its lack of basic facilities, and how she'd have enjoyed this new version. Here were all the latest labour-saving devices she could have wished for, from dishwasher to microwave to state-of-the-art coffee maker.

Yet at the same time the room still retained the cosy, lived-in feeling of an old-fashioned farmhouse kitchen. There was even, she saw with delight, a small black cat asleep in a Windsor chair next to the Aga — the same Aga that had been here in her father's time. She was absurdly pleased that Luke had kept it.

'Well, look at you.' Jenna bent down to stroke the cat's silken fur. The animal awoke, stretched, then jumped down from the chair and began to weave itself in and out of Jenna's legs, mewing appealingly.

'Are you trying to tell me it's dinner time?' Jenna laughed. 'Well, let me take this tea in, then we'll find out about the feeding schedule.'

But when she went in to Luke, he was asleep. She placed the tray quietly on the bedside table and looked down at him. It was strange how, with his eyes closed, he looked younger, far more vulnerable. A sick man trying to come to terms with a dreadful accident. This wasn't the man she'd hated for all those years, although she knew when those eyes opened, with their fierce, challenging gaze, that man would reappear.

She went back into the kitchen to be welcomed by the cat who, by now, had managed to convince itself that it hadn't been fed for a fortnight.

'You don't exactly look starved,' She laughed. 'But I'll feed you anyway.'

She'd just filled the dish when the phone rang. She snatched it up, something she'd got into the habit of doing when her mother was sleeping.

'Hello?' She hoped the phone hadn't disturbed Luke.

'Ah, wonderful!' the voice on the other end boomed. 'You must be Mrs Grantley. Mr Grantley said he was expecting you any moment. So pleased you finally made it. Such a relief because it's bad news, I'm afraid. But of course, not bad now you're there.'

'Look, I'm sorry,' Jenna began. 'Who's calling? I'm afraid I'm not — '

'So sorry. Such a fool, that's me. Too many things on my mind. Getting too old for this job. Should have been pensioned off years ago. I'm Sister Martin, District Nurse, and the bad news is that Mrs Otton, the lady I'd lined up to come and do for poor Mr Grantley, can't come. Her daughter's sick again. A fretful child — spends far too much time slumped in front of the TV instead of getting out in the fresh air, and — '

'Sister Martin; please tell me . . . ' Jenna cut across the flow. 'You said 'poor Mr Grantley'. I mean, he is . . . he's going to be all right, isn't he?'

Sister Martin sniffed. 'That's not for me to say. Maybe if you'd been by his bedside in hospital when he was low — very low indeed, I might tell you — instead of gallivanting around the world on a shopping trip,' she gave another loud sniff, 'the doctor could have explained things properly to you.

But I have to say, Mrs Grantley, things don't look too good at the moment. He should still be in hospital, of course, but he can be a difficult man as I'm sure you know.'

'Very difficult,' Jenna agreed with feeling. 'But Sister, there's something you ought to know — '

'Your private life is nothing whatsoever to do with me,' the nurse steamrollered on. 'But he was only allowed home because he assured them you'd be there; Mrs Grantley. Then when I called in this morning and found he didn't know when you'd be arriving — well, Brackwith is no place for a man in his condition to be on his own, which is why I organised Mrs Otton. Not ideal, but better than nothing. I must say, I feel much happier knowing that you'll be there twenty-four hours a day.'

'Does he need round-the-clock nursing?' Jenna was horrified at the prospect.

'Oh, no. And no dressings to deal

with now. Just plenty of rest. His legs are a mess, though, I'm afraid, particularly the right one. Multiple fractures, a terrible mess — and Mr Grantley's problem, as I'm sure you're aware, is himself. He has only a faint chance of regaining mobility — and that will be reduced to none whatsoever if he slips, takes a tumble or does anything that will put any pressure on those joints that are trying to heal.'

'Oh. That's not so good.' Jenna swallowed. 'I had no idea . . .'

Sister Martin's voice softened. 'No, well, maybe he didn't tell you the full story. I can well believe that. Hates a fuss, doesn't he? They make the worst patients, his sort.'

'I'm beginning to find that out,' Jenna agreed. 'But, look, I must tell you — '

'Sorry. That's my doorbell. Must dash. Waiting to borrow a Land Rover. Have to get up to an elderly hip fracture in Little Langdale. You're all right up there, aren't you? Mr Grantley told me he's enough provisions for a siege. I'll be up as soon as I can. Just make sure he rests. That's what he needs most of all at the moment. Plenty of rest.'

Jenna frowned as she replaced the receiver. Sister Martin hurled words at such a breakneck speed, it took a while for everything she'd said to sink in. She'd obviously believed her to be Luke's wife, for a start. That was the danger of answering someone else's phone. You ran the risk of being mistaken for the person the caller was expecting to hear.

There was also the risk of becoming involved in other people's problems. Jenna was quite prepared to fight Luke over what he'd done to her father, for her share of Brackwith and his plans to convert the place into a hotel. But how could she stand against a man who was as down as he was, having to fight his battles alone? What had Sister Martin said about his wife being off on a shopping trip? What sort of a woman was he married to, for Heaven's sake?

That question was answered, in part at least, when she went in to check if the telephone had disturbed him. A silver-framed photograph stood on one of the cupboards. Jenna looked at the lovely face that smiled out from the photograph. Who said the camera can't lie? Jenna expected some impeccably groomed, self-centred beauty, not this lovely young woman with the warm smile and laughing eyes, whom, under other circumstances, she felt she could have liked.

She looked down again at the sleeping figure on the bed. The battle between them wasn't over by a long way. Indeed, it had hardly begun but, for tonight at least, she needed a place to stay — and he needed her, although he'd probably deny it. Time to call a truce, however temporary.

She forced herself to remember how he'd abandoned her father in a snowstorm, just like the one outside, but the customary burning anger wouldn't come. Later, of course, it would return to haunt her as usual, but for now, the storm had created a kind of limbo and somehow, for once, she was content to live in the present moment.

Luke's last painkiller had a strong, sedative effect, for although he awoke when she brought him a light supper, his eyes were dull and distant. He registered little reaction to her decision to stay, apart from suggesting she took the bedroom on the right at the top of the stairs.

It had been her parents' room and she was uneasy about ghosts she might encounter there. But she needn't have worried. The room was very different from the cold, gloomy place it had been in their time. Now, it had ivory-coloured walls, pretty floral curtains, a bed with a brass bedstead and a beautiful, hand-worked quilt in shades of pinks and greens spread across it. There were no ghosts here to disturb her sleep.

* * *

During the past fortnight, when she'd been planning the trip north, Jenna had tried to imagine what it would be like for her to sleep at Brackwith again. She'd assumed the house would be dark, Spartan and cold, as it had been eleven years before.

Instead, here she was snuggled up in an extremely comfortable bed in a bright, centrally heated room — with a small black cat purring at her feet into the bargain.

In the morning she'd think about whether Luke had the right to make these changes to their joint property without consulting her. For the moment, though, she was very glad that he had.

She turned off the light, burrowed deep into the crisp cotton sheets and fell asleep immediately with no ghosts, only the small contented cat for company.

* * *

When she awoke next morning, Jenna lay still for a few minutes, trying to make sense of the unfamiliar surroundings. Then memory returned in a rush. She couldn't count the number of times she had dreamed she was back at Brackwith. But this time it hadn't been a dream. This time it had been for real. She really was back.

She looked out of the window, expecting to see everything carpeted in snow, but Luke had been right. This had, indeed, been one of those storms that had promised much but delivered little. Certainly, there was snow on the fells and the snow line extended considerably further down into the valley than it had done the day before, but the yard was clear. The snow had been piled up in corners of buildings and under hedges, as if swept there by a giant brush.

'That doesn't mean you've finished with us yet though, does it?' she said to the storm cloud that still clung to the top of Brackwith Pike, its heavy greyness now softened by the pink tinge of the early morning sun.

Behind the house was a sheer wall of rock known as Bob's Crag and in front of the Crag, a small field. She dressed and hurried outside, breathing in deep lungfuls of the crisp, clean air — the sort of air, her father used to say, that was so clean you could wash your face in it. She went into the field and looked up at the Crag. It was a dramatic rock face, but not difficult — in fact, ideal to learn on.

She saw herself not as she was now, grieving, unsettled and unhappy, but ten years old, secure and happy in the love of her adored father, desperate for him to teach her to climb. It had been a glorious morning in June and, like today, she'd woken early and gone out to the Crag. Her father had a group of students coming later and Jenna had begged to be allowed to join them. Her mother had said no.

'One climber in the family is enough,' she'd said. 'You're not to encourage her, John. You promised.'

Jenna could still feel her disappointment at her father's readiness to go along with her mother's wishes. Couldn't he see how desperately Jenna wanted to climb? How come he'd teach all the others, all those silly, gangly boys, and not his own daughter? It wasn't fair.

Well, if he wouldn't teach her, she'd teach herself. After all, she'd watched him climb the Crag often enough with those boys and if they could do it, so could she.

So she had embarked on her first attempt at rock climbing — but before very long she became stuck. She couldn't go up or down. She wasn't afraid; just annoyed with herself for not knowing what to do next.

From nowhere, her father had appeared beside her, telling her quietly and calmly what to do. Once she'd been shown the moves, it had seemed so obvious that she was furious with herself — as furious as she'd expected him to be when they both got safely back down.

But he hadn't been angry. Instead he'd said gently but firmly that from now on there'd be no more teach-yourself expeditions. Rock climbing, he'd said, was not something to be taken lightly and he'd teach her the safe and correct way.

'I didn't realise it meant so much to you,' he'd said, smiling down at her with those dark green eyes that were exact mirrors of her own.

'But Mum won't — '

'Don't you worry about your mother,' he'd said. 'I'll sort things out with her.'

True to his word, John had taught his daughter to climb and to share his love and respect for the mountains. He was an excellent instructor, patient yet firm, and she proved an apt pupil, if a touch over-adventurous at times. During that summer, Jenna got to know every inch of Bob's Crag and progressed to more challenging climbs on Brackwith Pike. It was a magical time — full of long sunny days and the promise of even better ones to come.

But then Fate had intervened. In late August of that year, Rob Williamson, one of her father's climbing companions and a great friend of the family, was killed in the Himalayas on an expedition that John should have been on but wasn't.

That event marked the beginning of the end of her parents' stormy marriage. Her mother, who had never been happy with John's climbing 'obsession', as she called it, went on and on at him, in a futile series of rows as she tried to persuade him to give up his beloved climbing.

Again and again, he had refused — although to Jenna's dismay and fury, he did agree to stop taking Jenna with him.

To her it was the ultimate betrayal. She had begged, cried, cajoled, raged at him, but in vain. He'd promised. No more climbing for Jenna until she was older.

'When?' she'd cried. 'After Christmas? Next summer? When I'm twelve?

When, Dad, when?'

'One day,' he said. 'I promise. Not yet, but one day.'

But 'one day' never came. As August dragged into September, the tension between her parents became unbearable. Arguments carried out in harsh, bitten-off whispers, uncomfortable silences where they ignored each other or acted like strangers, had all ended when Lynda had driven away from Brackwith with Jenna and James, never to return.

* * *

Jenna stumbled and put her hand out to save herself. She felt the rough surface of the rock graze her palm and was shocked to see that while she'd been engrossed in the past, her steps had taken her through the field and along the footpath to the foot of Bob's Crag.

She leaned back slightly to look up at the Crag towering above her.

There was her usual feeling of disbelief that she'd ever thought she enjoyed scrambling about its rocky face. But there was a glimpse, too, of another feeling. A flash of excitement and exhilaration — and a thrilling memory of being, quite literally, on top of the world.

Then she shook her head and walked back towards the house. Her mother had been right, of course. Climbing was just a way of getting to spend time with her father. She hated climbing — and climbers — more than anything else in the world. Just like her mother.

She let herself back into the house and stood for a while outside Luke's bedroom, listening for any sound that would signify he was awake. When none came, she opened the door to the study. She had to see if her father's presence that she'd felt so strongly yesterday was still there.

In this room he'd written several mountaineering books that had become classics, and Jenna saw with satisfaction that they were still in the same bookcase.

Her keen eye saw that another bookcase that used to be full of old magazines, broken binoculars and spare bootlaces now held books written by Luke Grantley.

The desk stood where her father had placed it, in front of the window looking towards the magnificent skyline dominated by Brackwith Pike.

She turned away, looking down at the litter of papers across the desk. What a mess. How on earth could he find — ?

She caught her breath and reached for the letter in her mother's unmistakable handwriting.

'What d'you think you're doing?'

Jenna whirled round, horrified to see Luke in the doorway, resting on a pair of elbow crutches. The expression on his face was as threatening as the snow cloud on top of Brackwith Pike.

5

'Mr Grantley! You startled me.' Jenna dropped her hand to her side and tried to make her voice sound natural. 'I thought Sister Martin said you had to rest?'

'Indeed she did.' He crossed the room with an ease that surprised her until she realised that he'd have a climber's well-developed upper body strength to enable him to handle crutches with comparative ease. 'However,' he went on, 'that does not necessarily mean bed rest.'

'I — I didn't realise you were so . . . so mobile,' she stammered. 'The wheelchair . . . '

'Forgive me for not being the helpless invalid you took me for,' he said icily as he made his way across the room. 'The wheelchair is only there because the damn fool paramedic refused to let me come across the yard on my crutches and insisted on leaving it there, 'just in case', even though I told him hell would freeze over before I got in it again.'

He looked quickly over the contents of his desk top. Jenna sent up a silent prayer of thanks that she hadn't had time to pick up her mother's letter, for she knew that brief but intense glance would have told him immediately if anything at all had been moved.

'Well?' His eyes were cold. 'You still haven't told me what you're doing in here.'

'Me? Well . . . to clean, of course. I thought I'd check in here first — you know, to see what needs doing.'

'But I distinctly remember telling you yesterday not to come in here.'

'I wasn't going to disturb anything, just vacuum the floor, that sort of thing.'

'Well, that won't be necessary.' He moved between her and the door, effectively blocking off any escape. 'Now, why not stop this nonsense and tell me what you're really doing here?'

'I . . . don't know what you mean.' Jenna took a couple of steps back, her heart thudding so wildly that she was sure he must be able to hear it.

'I think I've got a pretty good idea who you are, Miss Jane Bennington,' he said, still in that quiet, cold voice. 'And you're no cleaning lady, that's for sure.'

'Oh? And who — or is it what? — do you think I am?'

Jenna was proud of the way her voice sounded so steady, not even a small tremor to betray the panic churning inside her.

'I think you're a journalist.' He looked at her so fiercely that she took another step backwards, her hip colliding painfully with the edge of the bookcase as she did so. 'There's something familiar about you. And I'm sure we've met, or at least spoken quite recently. I know your voice, even though your name means nothing to me. Those damn pills have addled my brain at the moment but it'll clear. I don't usually forget a name and I'm willing to bet that Jane Bennington isn't yours.

'Am I right? Am I to be your next big exclusive? 'Famous novelist crippled for life in mountain accident'?'

'You're right about one thing, Mr Grantley. Those pills have addled your brain. Either that or you've been reading too many of your own novels. What is it you write? Fantasy adventures?'

Jenna turned towards the window. Any minute now, she thought, he'd remember the telephone conversation they'd had the day before her mother's funeral. It had been a short, bitter exchange and one neither of them was likely to forget. Even with her back to him, she was aware of him watching, still with that same intense gaze.

She looked up towards Brackwith Pike. What on earth was she going to say now? Wouldn't it be better to face up to it? To admit she'd been deceiving him, that she was in fact Jenna Manning?

Inside her head, she heard her father's voice, as clearly as if he was there in the room. *Don't give up now. You'll find the way if you just reach out for it.*

And so it was. Her father had been right. She had found the way forward — if she could only hold her nerve and follow it.

She took a deep, steadying breath.

'You're right in a way,' she said. 'But I'm not the kind of journalist you're thinking of. I'm freelance. I write feature articles and I'm researching one at the moment. However, it's not you I'm interested in, I'm afraid, but John Manning, the famous mountaineer who, I believe, once owned this place. He died about seven years — '

'Seven and a half,' Luke cut in, scowling. 'For pity's sake, you're not going to drag all that up again, are you?'

You bet your sweet life I am! Jenna thought. *But when we do sort this out, Luke Grantley, it'll be at my instigation, not yours. There are things going*

71

on here that I've a right to know about. But just for the moment, I have the edge on you, since I know who you are but you don't know who I am — yet. And I'm going to play that advantage for as long as I can.

She smiled with what she hoped was professional reassurance. 'I'm more interested in his achievements, people he helped, that sort of thing — '

'In that case, why pretend you're a cleaning lady?'

'I didn't pretend. You assumed that and didn't give me the chance to introduce myself. But to get back to John Manning. You said yesterday that coming here as a young boy changed your life. Do I take it that John Manning had something to do with that change?'

She held her breath while he appeared to struggle with himself over whether to answer her question or throw her out.

'Everything,' he said eventually. 'He had everything to do with it. Everything

I am — and everything I could have been but am not — I owe to John Manning.'

The change in him was remarkable. It was as if, having decided that she was who she'd said she was, he'd let go. The cold, hard look vanished; so, too, the lines of tension that had been etched deep into his cheeks. Instead, his face was relaxed, his eyes softer, as if he was looking back on something pleasant.

'I'd like to tell you about him,' he said. 'However, if I agree to talk to you, will you promise to let me see your copy before it's published? It's important you understand the kind of man you're writing about. His sort don't come along often. He was exceptional.'

She nodded. 'Of course I will,' she said, then, as he shifted his weight from one crutch to the other, Sister Martin's warnings came back to her. 'Your leg!' she exclaimed. 'I'm sure you shouldn't be standing on it. Why don't we go in to the kitchen and you can talk while I get breakfast?'

'I don't eat breakfast.'

'Well, I do,' she returned, leading the way. 'I walked to the foot of Bob's Crag this morning and I'm starving.'

'Bob's Crag? You must be local to call it that.'

Jenna was thankful that she reached the kitchen ahead of him and was able to busy herself searching for bread and locating the toaster before answering.

'Of course I call it Bob's Crag,' she called back down the passage, placing butter and marmalade on the scrubbed deal table as he hobbled in. 'I told you, I'm from Ambleside. And yes, I know the story of how it's named after a long-serving member of the Mountain Rescue team. Now, come on, tell me about how you met John Manning.'

'I was a bit of a tearaway when I first met John,' he said, helping himself to a slice of toast as she put down the plate. 'I was fourteen years old and had been in four different foster homes in four years.'

Jenna felt the pain behind his words

74

and felt a tug of sympathy. She had to keep reminding herself who she was talking to, and what he had done. Maybe the journalist cover story wasn't such a good idea after all.

'Do you mind me asking what happened to your parents?' she asked. 'Off the record, if you prefer.'

He shrugged. 'Dad was killed in a car crash when I was eight. Mum went to pieces and, like so many others, thought she'd found the answer at the bottom of a bottle. She managed to keep some sort of home together for a while, then gave up and took off, who knows where. Neither she nor Dad had much family, and those they did have didn't want to know me and my sister. Hence the foster homes.

'Mind you, I wasn't an easy kid. I hated the whole world and everyone in it. I don't blame them. Not now, although I did at the time. Some of them had rather — ' He hesitated, his expression grim as he searched for the right word. 'Let's say 'original' ideas when it came to ways of instilling discipline.'

He bit hard into his toast. 'I'm sorry. You want to hear about John, not my life story.'

'It sounds as if the two are linked,' she said. 'Do go on.'

'Well, needless to say, my hatred of the world included school. I played truant more often than I turned up but on one of the few times I did bother to go in, I was lucky enough to pick a day when John came to the school to give us a talk.

'Of course, I didn't want to be there so I sat at the back, arms folded, mind closed. But there was something about the way he spoke, the photographs he showed, that finally got through the barriers I'd put up around myself. So when at the end of the talk, he said he had a place in the Lake District and he'd take a group of us there in the summer holidays to try our hand at rock-climbing, I was first in the queue, much to everybody's amazement, including my own

— although not, as he told me later, his. He'd seen something in my face, he said, and that if I hadn't volunteered, he'd have dragged me there by the hair if necessary.'

Jenna handed him a mug of coffee in silence. She didn't want to interrupt his train of thought. She was also remembering how she used to grumble about those 'silly boys' her father used to bring to Brackwith. And how, if she was honest, she was jealous of the attention he gave them.

'Before I got halfway up my first climb I knew I'd found something that I'd been searching for all my life, without knowing I was looking, if that makes any sense.'

As he spoke, Luke's eyes glowed as if he was once again back on the mountains, looking up with anticipation towards a distant summit. 'John was a wonderful instructor,' he declared. 'I can't tell you what it felt like, that first time on Bob's Crag with him beside me.'

You don't have to, Jenna thought bleakly. *I remember.*

'After that,' Luke went on, 'John became a big part of my life. He arranged a foster home for me and my sister with a wonderful couple, who gave us the love and stability we so badly needed. He also made me see that I could make something of my life. He persuaded, bullied and pressured me to get my head down and get on with my schoolwork so that eventually I got my A-levels and went on to do a degree in geology at university. It was even John who got me writing. In short, he really was the father I never had.'

He was the father I never had, too! Jenna thought with anguish, recalling all the broken promises, the non-appearances when John had been busy with his latest book or away on yet another expedition. If a wife came a long way down a mountaineer's list of priorities, Jenna had discovered that his children came even further down that list — a fact her mother had never failed to point out with self-justifying relish.

And yet, he'd found time to — what had Luke said? — 'persuade, bully and pressure' the rebellious young Luke Grantley into making something of his life. She dwelt on that thought, as if probing an old wound to see if it hurt.

Of course it did. It still hurt agonisingly! The wound of losing the father she'd adored went deep, so deep she could still feel the pain of his desertion. She was jealous of the way he'd helped Luke when he'd never been there for her. Why hadn't he come to see her? Why hadn't he kept his promises?

Then, like a shaft of sunlight breaking through her black thoughts, she remembered the one promise he had kept — that, one day, she'd come back to Brackwith. Yes, the pain was still there, but maybe not quite as raw now. Maybe she'd been right to come here after all.

She looked up, aware that Luke had

finished speaking and was looking at her as if expecting a response.

'I'm sorry.' She decided that honesty — or at least, partial honesty — was best. 'Something you said triggered a memory and I was away down memory lane for a while.'

'I hope they were pleasant memories,' he said and his voice was so unexpectedly gentle that, to Jenna's horror, hot tears filled her eyes.

'No,' she whispered, eyes shimmering, 'They weren't. Oh no,' she dashed an angry hand across her eyes, 'I'm making an awful fool of myself. I never cry. I'm sorry.'

He reached across and took her hand away from her eyes. 'Don't apologise for your feelings,' he said softly. 'I'm sorry if it was something I said that caused your sadness.'

With unexpected tenderness, he brushed away the tear that trickled down her cheek. Jenna held her breath, afraid that anything as mundane as breathing would break the extraordinary spell. A tingle was spreading across her face from where he'd touched her and it felt as if champagne, not blood, was whizzing around her veins.

'Oh, Jane,' he said, in a gentle voice that beguiled her senses as he placed his hand over hers in a gesture of comfort. She looked down at their hands, hers palm up on the table, a small neat hand with long slender fingers; his strong and practical-looking, still bearing the cuts and bruises from his climbing accident.

Jane? He'd called her Jane. Was she Jane? Was it that, in pretending to be Jane Bennington, she'd somehow become her? Because Jenna Manning had certainly never had this reaction to a man's touch. Besides, this sort of thing didn't happen — at least, not outside the covers of a book.

Yet it was happening. With Luke Grantley, of all people. The man who'd left her father to die. The man who'd robbed her of her chance to put things right between them.

She stood up abruptly, almost knocking her chair over as she did so. 'Would you like some more toast?' she said. 'Because for someone who didn't want any breakfast, you've done a good job of demolishing the last lot.'

He looked as if her sudden movement had startled him and, for a brief second, there was a question in his eyes. Then he grinned at her.

'It must be that special way you have of making toast,' he returned. 'Obviously, you're a woman of many talents.'

Jenna flushed. 'Do go on with your story,' she said, feeling she'd be on safer ground if he went back to his memories, even though they were awakening painful ones of her own. 'Did you continue to see D — John Manning once you'd left school?'

Luke nodded. 'He got me some vacation work with one of his friends and I went climbing with him as often as that and my studies would allow. I spent as many weekends as I could up here, helping him do the place up. It was pretty rundown when he took it on. When the old man who'd farmed here died, his sons weren't interested so the place fell to bits. Leaking roof, no electricity, that sort of thing. John's marriage broke up about the time I met him, and what had been a weekend and holiday place then became his home.'

'He lived here at Brackwith, all the time?' Jenna was stunned. 'I didn't know.'

'Where else could he live?' Luke's voice had a harsh edge. 'His wife took him to the cleaners, determined he'd keep her in the manner she'd decided she was entitled to. As for his kids — ' He scowled. 'Nothing but the best for them. Music lessons, private school, trips abroad. Everything they wanted and then some. They wanted for nothing.'

Jenna wished she could stop him, that she could shut out what he was saying. Or even tell him he'd got it all wrong, surely. And yet, it was true they'd been comfortably off and had never had to forego a school trip or special treat because of lack of funds. She'd always assumed her father had enjoyed a similar standard of living.

'They lacked a father,' she pointed out.

Luke stirred his coffee furiously. 'That was their choice,' he snapped, brows drawn together in an angry frown. 'To them he was just the guy with the cheque book. They didn't want to know him, otherwise.'

'What makes you say that?' Jenna's heart was thudding. She didn't want to hear any more. Yet she had to know.

'Because I was with him on more than one occasion when he was getting ready for a visit from them, full of plans of where they'd go, what they'd do. But every single time without fail, his wife would phone at the last minute. They couldn't — or more likely wouldn't — come. Eventually, of course, he stopped asking. But he never stopped missing them, especially his daughter, his precious Jenna.'

6

The coffee cup slipped from Jenna's fingers and crashed to the floor. She wanted to scream that he'd got it all wrong, to tell him what it was really like.

Instead, she murmured, 'Do go on,' as she bent down to pick up the broken cup, thankful that mopping up the spilt coffee enabled her to hide her face.

'He adored both his children,' Luke said. 'But he had a special soft spot for Jenna, the eldest. Before the divorce, she'd been a bright, lively kid, full of adventure — a natural climber, John said, and he was usually right about things like that.

'Apparently, he'd begun to teach her to climb when she was about ten and she took to it like a duck to water. But her mother hated anything to do with mountains — a bit like you, I suppose?

85

— and insisted that he stopped encouraging her until she was old enough to make up her own mind. But as she got older, she lost interest. There was always something more important to her than visiting him. He'd spend hours poring over routes, always planning with her in mind. 'D'you think Jenna would like this?' or 'This'll tempt Jenna back into a pair of climbing boots, I'll bet you anything you like.' Lucky for him I never took the bet.' Luke's eyes had darkened again. 'Poor devil. That wretched girl broke his heart.'

Jenna shivered. She was peering over the edge of a precipice, watching her familiar world tilting and distorting in front of her. She couldn't make sense of it. She wanted to tell him it hadn't been the way he said — that he'd only seen things from her father's viewpoint. But she could still feel the anger radiating off him in waves. She knew she was being a coward, but she needed space to confront the conflicting emotions that raged inside her head.

She wasn't yet ready to face his withering contempt. Not until she'd marshalled some sort of defence for herself. She needed time. Just time.

With one of those mercurial mood changes she was beginning to recognise as typical of Luke, his anger vanished and he leaned across towards her and smiled.

'Hey, don't look so sad,' he said. 'It all happened a long time ago and is not relevant in an article about John's achievements. He was intensely loyal to his children, wouldn't hear a word against them. He'd never forgive me if I went on record saying all that, whatever I feel about them personally. So, that last bit was strictly off the record, okay? Forget I said it.'

'It's forgotten,' she lied. 'It's just that . . . well, don't you think that mountaineers, successful ones like John Manning, put an awful strain on their families? The separations, the constant fear that each parting could be the final one? Don't you think that's a pretty selfish way of living your life?'

He glared across the table at her. 'Is that the line your article is going to take?'

'I'm not 'taking any line', as you put it. I'm trying to tell the whole truth about the man. From what you tell me about him, I'm sure that's what he'd have wanted, too.'

Luke shrugged and drained the last of his coffee. 'Maybe. I had this idea of writing John's biography. I'm amazed nobody else has done it before now. I approached his widow but she didn't want to know.'

'Well — perhaps she just thought you weren't the right person to do it.'

'And you obviously don't either, judging from your tone,' he said, hostility sharpening his voice. 'May I ask why?'

'Well, perhaps you were, or still are, too close. It's hard then to be as objective as you should be. You were with him on his last expedition, I believe?'

There! She'd done it! She held her breath as Luke looked at her, his eyes unflinching. Jenna lifted her chin and returned his gaze. The silence hung, as heavy and threatening as a storm cloud between them, the only sound being the hiss of the kettle singing quietly to itself on the Aga.

'This isn't going to work, is it? I think you've asked enough questions and I've certainly answered all I'm going to. You'd better go before the weather turns bad again.' He pulled himself to his feet, his crutches clattering against the table leg as he did so. 'Let yourself out and — '

He got no further. As before, his face turned a sickening grey and beads of sweat appeared on his brow. His face contorted as the spasm shook his body and he cursed violently through clenched teeth.

'Have you had your painkillers today?' she asked, her concern for him overriding any other emotion.

He shook his head. 'Trying . . . to cut

. . . cut them . . . out,' he managed to say.

'Not very successfully, by the look of you. And way too soon. Come on. Back to bed.'

By the time she'd helped him back into bed, handed him the tablets and held the glass of water for him, Jenna had her feelings under control. Whatever was going on, whatever the truth about her father, whatever she felt about Luke, all that would have to wait. There was no way she was going to leave him alone in this isolated place in his present condition.

'I thought . . . I thought I told . . . you to . . . to go.' It took enormous effort for him to force out the words.

'And I told Sister Martin I'd stay, so that's what I'm doing. And you'll have to put up with it, because to put it bluntly, you're not in a position to do anything else, are you?'

He scowled but said nothing. She smoothed the pillows and saw with relief the clenched muscles gradually relax and a more natural colour return to his face.

'Look, I'm sorry if my questions upset you,' she went on, 'My mother always used to tell me off for saying the first thing that came into my head, without thinking it through. I'm going to ring Sister Martin and she'll — '

She clapped her hand to her mouth and looked at him with eyes filled with horror. 'Sister Martin! I completely forgot. She's made a terrible mistake. She thinks I'm your wife. I tried to explain, but you must know what she's like. I couldn't get a word in on the phone — '

'I thought you told me yesterday that Sister Martin had sent you.' His eyes were alert now and full of suspicion. 'If that's true, how come she mistook you for my wife?'

'It was you who made assumptions about who I was, the same as Sister Martin did,' Jenna retorted. 'I came here yesterday on the off-chance. In fact, I only came to look around the

91

place and didn't expect to find anyone here.'

She was congratulating herself on having almost told the truth when she saw with horrifying clarity that his next question was going to be, 'How did you get in?' She hurried on, hoping to fend it off. 'Sister Martin was relieved when I answered the phone. Mind you — ' she forced a laugh — 'I got quite a ticking-off from her for not having been at your bedside sooner. A woman's place, and all that.'

For one unguarded second, Jenna saw an expression of such intense loneliness flash across his face that she cursed herself for the flippant remark.

'Oh Luke, I'm so sorry,' she whispered. 'I shouldn't have joked about it.'

The revealing show of emotion was gone as quickly as it had come and his face became closed and defensive. In that look she saw a glimpse of the prickly young boy he'd been before he met her father. A wary, suspicious young boy, always being pushed into second place by uncaring foster parents, now a grown man yet still receiving similar treatment — but this time from his wife.

'So why isn't your wife here?' She was surprised at how indignant she felt on his behalf.

'What is this?' he snapped. 'More dirt for your article?'

'Of course not. I wouldn't do something like that.'

'How on earth would I know what you would or wouldn't do when I don't even know who you are?' he said, in a deceptively quiet voice that sent an icy trickle down her back.

Now! a voice inside her head urged her. *Tell him now. Tell him you're Jenna Manning, he'll tell you to go to hell and then you can walk away from all this. You can keep all your illusions, too, all your fantasies about how badly your father treated you. That way you'll never have face the uncomfortable truth about how badly you treated him. Tell him now, Jenna, and then run away from here as fast as you can!*

She cleared her throat. 'I told you. I'm Jane Bennington. Now, if you'll excuse me, I must go and phone Sister Martin.'

'There's no need.'

'There's every need. She said I was to call her to let her know you're all right and still taking your medication. And — '

'Jane. Listen for a moment. Please.' His anger had disappeared, his voice had softened. 'Before you make that call, I — well, there's something I need to ask you. I was wondering if you'd do something for me?'

'That depends.' Jenna was suspicious of this latest sudden mood change. 'What is it?'

'Will you be my wife?'

'*What?*' This was the last thing in the world she'd expected him to say. 'Is this a joke? Or have the pills finally got to you?'

He shook his head, exasperated with himself. 'Sorry, that was a silly way of putting it. What I meant was, would you let Sister Martin go on thinking you're my wife?'

'But why on earth would I do that?'

'I got discharged from hospital only because I told them there'd be somebody here to look after me. Absolute nonsense, of course, because as you can see I'm quite capable of looking after myself.'

Jenna thought of how she'd had to help him back into bed, his body contorted with pain, his face that awful grey colour. But she said nothing.

'Julia is abroad at the moment,' he went on. 'She's a buyer for Up Front Fashion House. This trip is really important to her. It could well be the big break she — '

'She's buying *clothes?*' Jenna shared Sister Martin's indignation. 'She's off on a jolly, buying clothes, while you're — you're lying here — '

'Will you do it?' His voice, as he cut across her, was like ice. 'A simple yes or no will do. Spare me the lecture and I'll spare you hearing me tell you to mind your own business.'

'Yes, but — '

'Good. Now, if you don't mind, I'm exhausted and, as I'm sure Sister Martin told you, I need plenty of rest.'

With that, he leaned back against the pillows, closed his eyes and went to sleep, or at least appeared to do so.

'But I didn't mean 'yes' as in 'yes I'd do it',' she protested. 'I meant, 'yes but — ''

She gave up when she realised she'd been outmanoeuvred. Short of shaking him by the shoulders and demanding he wake up and listen to her, there was nothing she could do.

She sighed and went off to call Sister Martin, promising herself that she wouldn't tell an outright lie, but realising that, if the conversation with Sister Martin went anything like the way it had done the day before, she probably wouldn't get much chance to tell her the truth about who she was, anyway.

She wasn't wrong. Like their previous

discussion, the conversation proved to be very one-sided and, apart from another passing reference to the elderly hip fracture in Little Langdale, entirely focussed on Luke's needs and medication.

It wasn't until she'd replaced the receiver, her ears still ringing from Sister Martin's machine-gun chatter, that she thought of using Luke's landline to call her brother. The mobile signal was virtually non-existent up here and she didn't think he'd mind.

But then, even if he did — she thought back indignantly to the way he'd just steamrollered her into deceiving Sister Martin — it was too bad.

★ ★ ★

'Jenna!' The relief with which James spoke her name made her feel guilty for having left it so long before contacting him. 'Are you all right? I phoned the hotel and they said you'd checked out yesterday. I thought you were going to stay there for a few days. Where are you?'

'I'm sorry. I should have called earlier. I'm at Brackwith.' She heard James's sharp intake of breath and hurried on before he could interrupt. 'It's . . . er . . . it's been done up a bit since we were last here and it's not too bad at all. In fact, I'm thinking of staying here for a few days. But why did you call the hotel? Is anything wrong?'

'Not wrong as such, although it does sound as if it's pretty urgent. Steven phoned me. Apparently he's been trying to get hold of you and is worried because he keeps getting your voice-mail.'

'The mobile signal is lousy around here. I'm using a landline at the moment. What did Steven want? Did he say?'

'Something about some job in London that he was talking to you about the other day? And that you'd said you needed to think about it? I told him you were up in the Lake District.

Will you call him? Or would you like me to pass on this number to him?'

'No!' she answered quickly. 'Don't do that. I'm still thinking about the job.'

It wasn't strictly true, she realised guiltily. Since that day in Mr Bennington's office when she'd learned about her father's will and Brackwith, she'd hardly given Steven and his job offer a thought.

'Well, don't take too long.' James's voice became unusually serious. 'Steven said something about needing to know pretty soon. I got the feeling, somehow, that he wasn't just talking about the job offer either.'

★ ★ ★

Jenna was unsettled after her conversation with James. Steven. Dear, kind Steven. He'd been her boss until, six months ago, he'd been headhunted by a company in London. They'd been out together a few times before he left and had stayed in touch. When she told him she was giving up her job in Bristol to look after her mother, he'd been wonderfully understanding and supportive and promised he'd keep his eye out for an opening in London for her. And he'd been as good as his word. When he came down to Somerset for her mother's funeral, he told her the job was as good as hers if she was interested in making a fresh start.

'I realise you don't want to be making any decisions right now,' he'd said gently. 'I just wanted you to know that the job is here for you if you want it. As, of course, am I. Just don't take too long making up your mind, eh?'

What to do about Steven? Like James, she realised he was offering her more than a job in London and it was unfair not to give him a straight answer. But she couldn't think of her future yet, not while the past was still crowding in on her.

If she could just get her head straight — about her father, about Luke. Everything had been so clear-cut before. She, her mother and James had all been victims of her father's selfishness; of Luke's callousness. Goodies versus baddies. Black versus white.

She prowled around the still house, going from room to room, thinking of her father living here alone after the divorce. Had he been happy? Had he ever thought of her and James, and wondered if they were happy? Luke had mentioned how he'd planned for her visits, worked out routes to tempt her back into a pair of climbing boots. But surely . . . ? She shook her head and pushed the thoughts aside.

She opened the door to the small, dark room that had once been her bedroom and caught her breath. Like the study downstairs, this room hadn't changed since she'd last been in it — but, unlike the study, it had lain empty and unused and had an abandoned feel to it. There was no mattress on the narrow, iron-framed bed and a cupboard door hung at an awkward angle on broken hinges.

Something showed faintly in the darkness of the cupboard. What was it? Something she'd left behind, that dreadful day they left? She pulled out a parcel, wrapped in green shiny paper, brushed the dust away and stared in disbelief as she uncovered a label in her father's handwriting.

It simply said: *To Jenna*.

The memory of that last, awful conversation she'd had with her father was seldom far from her consciousness. Now it rushed back to torment her and she tore feverishly at the wrapper, as if whatever it contained could blot it out.

Inside was a black oblong case and a letter addressed to her. The case lay on the floor beside her as she opened the envelope and read the short note.

The date was a very significant one. Even now, after all these years. It was the day of a school concert at which, unusually for her, she was playing a clarinet solo.

Both Jenna and James had inherited their mother's love of music. James was a gifted musician and shone in their school, which had a proud musical tradition. He had been performing solos in school concerts since he was old enough to hold a violin but for Jenna, the chance to take a solo part in the school concert had meant an awful lot to her.

I hope this reminds you of your great triumph, which I know tonight is going to be for you, darling girl. I'll be the proudest man in the hall tonight, that's for sure, her father had written.

I hope, too, that your mother was right and that this is the one you wanted — and that every time you play it, you'll think of me and maybe one day keep the promise you made, to come to the Concert Hall at Brackwith and play just for me and the chickens. They're still here, Jenna. Waiting for you. As am I. Don't leave it too long. See you soon. Love, Dad.

See you soon. He always finished every conversation, every letter with those words. *See you soon.* Only this time, those three words were heartbreaking in their irony, for she never did see him again. In spite of his promise to be there, he never came to the concert. And two months after writing the note that had never been sent, he went on an expedition with Luke Grantley and had not returned.

With shaking fingers, she undid the metal fastenings of the squat black case, knowing what she'd find inside. The clarinet rested, black and silver, against the blue velvet-lined box. She picked out each piece and fitted them together before inserting the mouthpiece. The instrument felt smooth and cold beneath her fingers and the keys moved easily.

She selected a reed, wetted it then set it into the mouthpiece. Would it still be playable after all these years? Probably not. Her fingers caressed the warm, smooth wood, pressed against the cold silver of the keys. Could she still remember the way to position her mouth, the correct way to breathe, deep from the diaphragm? Remember the correct amount of pressure to apply? She drew breath.

The first notes were strident. They made her wince but she made adjustments, and persevered. Gradually, the sounds became mellower as her confidence began to return, surprised at how much she remembered. She closed her eyes and dragged notes from deep within her and gradually relaxed as she began to enjoy the music.

As she finished, she felt her father's presence so strongly she could hear him clapping. She whirled round, the smile dying on her lips. For the sound didn't come from her emotionally charged imagination.

It was real. A slow, ironic handclap.

'That was quite a performance, Jenna Manning.' Luke's eyes were as cold and hard as flint. 'But then, that's what you're best at, isn't it — putting on a performance?'

7

The charade was over at last. Jenna felt only relief as she lowered the clarinet with exaggerated care and turned to face Luke. She wasn't going to apologise, nor be intimidated by him. She straightened up slowly and returned his gaze.

'What was the point of all that play-acting?' he asked. 'Come to check up on your inheritance? You could have come sooner, you know. After all, there was no danger of running into John, was there?'

She flinched at his cruel remark but said nothing. This was much more how she'd always imagined their first meeting, full of mutual hostility and recrimination. This she had rehearsed, time and again. This she could handle.

'Well?' He'd braced himself against the door frame, but transferred his weight to his crutches as he came towards her. 'What fiction is your creative mind working on now? Tell me, what is your real job? I've already rumbled the cleaning lady and I don't buy feature writer either.'

'I'm an accountant. Or, to be strictly accurate, a trainee. I had just completed my second year when Mum became ill.'

'I don't believe it!' Luke laughed, but it was a harsh sound without any humour in it. 'The daredevil, madcap Jenna Manning, an accountant? What on earth happened?'

This time she chose not to answer his question but instead asked one of her own. 'How did you know who I was?'

'It wasn't hard,' he said. 'In fact, I can't believe how long it took me to catch on. As I said before, those blasted pills have turned my brain to mush, but everything's beginning to clear now. How did I know? For a start, we've spoken on the phone recently and although our conversation was brief,' Jenna had to steel herself not to back away as anger lit his eyes, 'I knew your voice was familiar.

'Then there's your appearance. I can't believe how slow I was. You have John's hair colour and your eyes are a dead giveaway. They're so much like his — except, of course, their expression. John never glowered the way you're doing now.'

'I don't — !' Jenna began but Luke was not to be interrupted.

'But it was the music,' he went on. 'When I heard that, I knew for sure.'

'How do you mean?'

'The music you were playing. I recognised a bit of it. John had a tape of you playing that very piece at some concert or other. He was that proud of it, played it all the time, around the house, in the car. It drove me mad.'

'A tape? Of me? How did he get that?'

Luke shrugged. 'Your mother, I suppose. Maybe she felt sorry for him when she saw how upset he was after you'd asked him not to come to the school concert — '

Jenna gasped. 'What did you say?'

'I said maybe your mother — '

'No. After that, you said — you said *I asked him* not to come to the concert?'

She braced herself against the pain of reliving the memory of the night of the concert, her bitter disappointment as she'd watched every seat in the hall fill up. Every one, that is, except for the one next to her mother. She heard again her mother's words: 'Well, he only said he'd *try* to get here. But you know how unreliable he is and that he doesn't really like classical music. I told you not to get your hopes up, didn't I?'

Luke glared at her, misinterpreting her silence. 'For God's sake, don't you even remember? Then let me remind you.' His voice was harsh. 'Apparently, this concert was very important and you felt your father's presence would put you off, make you too nervous — afraid he'd clap in the wrong place, something like that.'

'No!' Jenna sat down heavily on the

narrow bed, oblivious of the pain as the iron frame cut into the backs of her legs. 'No. Oh, no. That wasn't how it was,' she whispered, speaking more to herself than to him. 'I wanted him to be there more than anything in the world but he . . . he said he'd probably not be able to make it — had to do some book signing, I think it was. I kept looking for him, all through the concert in case he was late, but he never came.'

'There was no book signing,' Luke said. 'I was here with him at the time, so I know. That's when he bought you that.' He indicated the clarinet, which Jenna grasped like a drowning woman clinging to a lifebelt. 'He was so looking forward to giving it to you. There was no way he'd have missed that — particularly for a book signing, which he hated doing anyway and would always wriggle out of if he could.'

'But he said . . . ' Her voice trailed away as a terrible suspicion dawned. Too terrible to contemplate.

She wouldn't have. Would she?

'Go on, then. What did he say?' Luke prompted. 'And to whom? You — or your mother?'

That was the suspicion she'd pushed aside when it first wormed its way into her head. But now Luke had put it into words, it refused to go.

Nevertheless, she refused to believe it.

'My mother.' She formed the words reluctantly. 'He said it to my mother. He phoned while I was out and I — I never got to speak to him.'

'And I suppose it was your mother who told John you didn't want him at the concert?'

'Oh no. She wouldn't — '

She broke off. She'd thought, back in Mr Bennington's office when she and James found out about Brackwith and their father's will, that she'd discovered the reason for her mother's anxiety in the weeks before she'd died. She knew something was troubling her and assumed, with hindsight, that it was because her mother had felt guilty

111

about not telling her about Brackwith sooner.

But what if it had been this? What if, for reasons best known to herself, it had been her mother who'd stopped her father from attending the concert?

But why? Why would she do such a terrible thing?

The concert had been a turning point in Jenna's relationship with her father. Or, more accurately, it had been the end of it. From then she'd forced herself to expect nothing from him and she'd stopped giving anything of herself in return. After the concert, when her mother hinted he'd probably had no intention of being there, she'd stood, dry-eyed and angry, and vowed she'd never let him get close enough to hurt her again.

So she made a point of turning down every invitation, of talking to him on the phone only when she really had to — and then with cold politeness, as if he were a stranger who meant nothing to her.

She looked down at the letter in her hands. If only she'd faced him, shouted at him, screamed at him. If only . . .

A strange sound filled the small room, the low keening of a creature in pain. Jenna looked round, and was stunned to realise it came from her.

'I didn't know,' she cried. 'I didn't know. If only I'd said something. If only I'd known — '

Luke shifted on his crutches and she saw that the expression on his face had changed from hostility to — what? Regret? Embarrassment? Or, was it, Heaven help her, pity?

She stood up, straightened her back, lifted her chin. She didn't want pity, least of all from Luke Grantley, of all people.

'Jenna,' he began, 'I — '

She turned towards him, her breathing rapid but her gaze steady, as was her voice.

'Spare me your sympathy,' she said coldly. 'After all, I'm Jenna Manning, remember? The girl who had everything she wanted and then wanted more? Well, I don't want anything from you — least of all sympathy.'

Luke's eyes darkened. 'I wasn't offering it,' he said curtly as he turned to go. 'Nor am I about to apologise for anything I said. People who listen at keyholes shouldn't complain if they hear things they don't like — and your play-acting was eavesdropping of the worst sort.'

'I wasn't eavesdropping — '

'Then what the devil do you call it? And, while we're discussing your little deception, what were you doing at my desk? Don't insult me by still insisting you were tidying it.'

'I saw a letter in my mother's handwriting.' In spite of her defiant words, she felt like a child caught with her hand in the biscuit tin. 'Naturally, I was curious.'

'Naturally?' His hostile stare held hers and Jenna was the first to look away.

'Oh, go to hell!' she snapped as the

strain of the morning took its toll. 'Of course her handwriting would catch my eye. She's just died, or had you forgotten? I see her every time I go out, you know. Someone with a similar way of moving their head, or wearing her sort of clothes or with her way of lifting her voice at the end of a sentence so that, for a moment, I think it is her. Of course I'd be drawn to her handwriting.

'But I don't understand why she was writing to you. Was it to do with Dad's biography?'

Luke laughed. Once again, it was that harsh, humourless laugh. 'Oh no,' he said. 'She ignored those letters. Couldn't be bothered to answer them. No, there was only one subject guaranteed to bring a response from Lynda Manning.'

Even as she asked the question, Jenna knew she wasn't going to like the answer. 'And that was?'

'Money.' he spat the word out, as if it had left an unpleasant taste in his mouth, and in spite of herself she recoiled from the contempt in his eyes.

'Money? You think she wanted money in exchange for details for my father's biography?' She gave a shaky laugh, relieved now she knew he was wrong. 'Now you're being ridiculous. She'd never do something like that.'

Luke turned towards her and the careless movement caused a spasm of pain. Jenna made a move towards him but checked herself, warned off by the expression in his eyes. The anger between them went too deep to be put aside, even for his pain. She hardened herself to stand back without offering help as he struggled against it.

'You should be in bed,' she said. The only response she got was a soft but violent curse, but whether this was aimed at her or the pain, she neither knew nor cared.

After what seemed hours but had in fact only been seconds, Luke regained control. His skin was grey and the bruise on his cheek more livid than ever. But his eyes were clear, his voice was steady. He took a deep breath and leaned back against the door frame.

'It wasn't anything to do with your father's biography,' he said, only a slight shortness of breath betraying what he had just endured. 'I told you, she ignored that. Our correspondence centred around the fact she was determined to drive up the price of her share in Brackwith.'

'*Her* share in Brackwith? But I — '

'Give me strength!' Luke sounded like a man at the end of his patience. 'For pity's sake, woman, will you stop this? Are you telling me you knew nothing about your mother's so-called negotiations? She knew how much this place meant to me and so the price kept going up and up. Now, you're an intelligent, well-educated young woman — an accountant, didn't you say? — so don't insult me by pretending you knew nothing about it, because I don't believe you.'

He held up a warning hand as Jenna drew breath to protest. 'In fact, now I come to think about it, this was probably all your idea, hence all the cloak-and-dagger stuff yesterday. Well, let me get one thing clear — the offer I made through our respective solicitors was my final one. Take it or leave it. I've done with it.'

Jenna sat, too stunned to speak, as he hefted himself back on to his crutches, steadied himself for a moment without the support of the door frame, then stumped along the landing, the rubber tips of his crutches thudding against the stripped floorboards. She listened, hardly daring to breathe as he made his way down the narrow, winding staircase. Once again, she was reminded of the tremendous upper body strength he had gained over the course of years of climbing and which enabled him to move with such apparent ease on the unwieldy crutches.

* * *

118

What now? Sitting by the narrow window, on the same small wooden chair on which she'd sat many times before, she read and re-read her father's letter until she knew each word by heart. But still she could make no sense of it.

Had her mother really deceived her that night, manipulated her into turning her back on her father? If that were true, it was a monstrous thing to do.

No — surely it was something Luke had made up to hurt her. But, if that was so, what about her father's letter? It read as if he had every intention of coming to the concert, so why . . . ?

She leaned forward, rested her elbows on the window ledge and gazed out at the view that had been so familiar and dear to her as a child. The room was directly above her father's study and enjoyed the same dramatic view, across the broad, sheep-dotted flanks of Brackwith Fell up to its highest point, where the soaring, grey cliffs of Brackwith Pike stretched towards the sky.

Because of the snow, Jenna could see clearly the part of the route known as Tig's Rake. It was a treacherous route in places but looked deceptively easy from this angle.

Was that where Luke fell?

She shuddered and turned away, her sombre mood echoed by the thick cloud that, even as she watched, rolled along the ridge and blotted out the summit.

Did she want to stay here and do battle with Luke over Brackwith? Did she want to live, quite literally, in the 'shadow of the high mountain'?

She thought not. There were ghosts here after all at Brackwith — ghosts that would have been better left undisturbed.

She closed the door on the small, sad room in the hope that by doing so, she could close the door on the small, sad child she had been. Ahead beckoned a new life, safe and predictable. Perhaps with Steven in London; perhaps a return to her old job and flat in Bristol. She wasn't sure yet. But whatever she did, wherever she went, the one thing she was sure about was that it would be as far away as possible from mountains and mountaineers.

If she went now, she'd have better memories of her father, thanks to his letter, whilst safeguarding her memories of her mother. They'd become closer during the last months of her illness, a closeness that had never been there during Jenna's childhood — when James had always been the favoured one — and she treasured it. She couldn't believe the person she'd mourned these last few weeks was capable of such cruel machinations.

She pushed the thought away and went downstairs. Luke had gone back to his study or bedroom, and she had no intention of disturbing him until she was ready to leave. Luke could do what he liked with Brackwith.

She'd go straight to the solicitor in Kendal, sign over her share and then she'd never have to see Luke again. There was nothing here for her now, and instinct told her that if she stayed much longer, she might discover things about her mother she'd rather not know.

It was the coward's way out — but Jenna was not prepared to take the risk.

8

There was, however, one thing she had to do before she left Brackwith for the last time. She took out her father's letter, reread it, then picked up her clarinet.

As she crossed the cobbled yard towards the barn, a few flakes of snow drifted down, vanishing into nothingness as they touched the ground. She turned her face towards the wintry sky and felt snowflakes melt against her skin like soft kisses. The wind had dropped and the air felt crisp. She breathed the sharp, cold air deep into her lungs and felt her troubled head begin to clear a little.

The big double door of the barn, not quite as large as she remembered, swung open easily on recently replaced hinges. Her father's study, whilst retaining the essence of what it had been in her father's time, had evolved with Luke's use of it. But as she stood in the barn, looking up at the high, beamed ceiling, she was ten years old again, gazing about with excitement. Nothing, but nothing, had changed.

It had thick stone walls and a dirt floor, packed solid from hundreds of years of use. Ancient wooden hay rakes, hessian sacks and discarded head collars used by long-dead horses still hung from pegs on the rough white-washed walls. And in a dark corner, hanging from yet more pegs . . . would they still be there?

Yes! Jenna gave a yelp of excitement as she reached into the gloom and found three old bikes, rusty and festooned with cobwebs, ranging in size from the largest, her mother's, to the smallest, her brother's. She smiled at the thought that her six-foot-plus brother could ever have sat on such a tiny thing. Yet he had, of course — although he'd never enjoyed careering around on a bike the way Jenna had.

'The bikes,' she murmured. 'The fun we used to have on them. Such good times.'

She smiled at an image of herself, bumping and rattling down the steep stony track, feet on the handlebars, red plaits streaming out behind her, daring a less than eager James to follow her.

But her smile died as the pictures moved on a few fateful minutes and now her mother's eyes, wild and blazing hatred, stared at her. She looked at James's small bike and saw that the dent was still there. He'd come careering down after her, lost his nerve half way and crashed into the dry-stone wall.

Poor James. Like the bike, he too bore the marks of that encounter and still had the horseshoe-shaped scar on his forearm. Now Jenna had total recall of every harsh word her mother had said, words that she'd succeeded in burying in her subconscious mind until now.

'You're a hateful, wicked girl,' her

mother had screamed, white-faced with shock as she'd tried to staunch the blood from the deep wound in James's arm. 'You did that deliberately. I saw it all. You goaded him into following, hoping he'd fall off, if I know you. You're a horrible girl, jealous of your little brother because he's everything you're not. He's clever, talented and good-looking, whereas *you* — '

Jenna heard no more because at that moment her father had arrived on the scene and taken control. The wound to James's arm was not as serious as it had first looked, although it needed several stitches, of which James was incredibly proud. Her mother had calmed down and behaved in a conciliatory manner towards Jenna, as if she regretted her outburst.

But it was too late. Jenna had seen the expression in her eyes. The damage had been done. James was the lucky one, his wound had been physical and soon healed, but for Jenna the memory of her mother's hate-filled eyes haunted her young life for many years.

Although Lynda Manning had never said anything quite so cruel again, there was a coldness in her dealing with her daughter that was never there with James.

James was, indeed, the centre of her mother's universe, the light of her life, whereas Jenna had always found herself hovering somewhere around the edges. So had she resented James? She certainly didn't hate him, but had her mother been right about her being jealous of him?

She tried to remember. Certainly she didn't envy him his musical talent and would never have wanted to put in the long hours of practice that he had done — and was still doing. And, while her father was around, she'd never minded James getting so much of her mother's attention.

But, maybe, later on — after her father had dropped out of their lives?

'You're exactly like your father,' was the phrase her mother would trot out if

Jenna displeased her. When her parents had tried to explain to them the reason for their divorce, that they'd stopped being married because they didn't love each other any more, Jenna's young mind had been quick to make the connection. Her mother didn't love her father. Jenna was like her father. Therefore, her mother didn't love Jenna any more. Hadn't she seen the proof of that with her own eyes?

She shivered forlornly. Another wretched ghost had reached across the years to her, reminding her of things and feelings better left buried. Was there nothing about Brackwith that evoked happy memories for her? Even the bikes, which she'd thought would bring forth only happy images, had unlocked things best forgotten.

From the farthest corner of the barn came the sound of a small red hen scratching at the floor, sending showers of dust and scraps of hay flying out in fussy little sprays behind her. This was the special place her father had mentioned, laughingly referred to as Brackwith Concert Hall. Here, at last, surely, she'd found somewhere that held only happy memories.

She shook off her gloom, smiled bravely and crossed to the part they'd called 'The Stage'. Here, Jenna and James had put on concerts and plays, the audience being made up of their parents, the family dog, the farm cats and as many sheep and chickens as wandered in.

She pulled two bales of hay into position, took out the clarinet and fitted it together again. This time, there was only one small red hen as her audience — except, maybe, for mice scuttling in dark corners. And, of course, her father. She'd come to keep her promise.

'This is for you, Dad,' she whispered as she closed her eyes, placed the clarinet to her lips then slowly, softly began to draw out the haunting notes of the second movement of Mozart's Clarinet Concerto. At first, her playing was hesitant and she faltered several times. She found it almost impossible to maintain the necessary control over her breathing as the emotion of the last few hours coursed through her.

Furious with herself, she stopped in mid-phrase, cutting off the music with a discordant sound.

'It's no good.' she said to the small red hen, who stopped scratching to raise her head in a beady stare. 'It's been too long and I can't get the breathing right. I can't do it.'

Yes, you can, Jenna. Her father's voice inside her head was as real to her as if he had been sitting in front of her in 'the stalls', as he used to. *You can do anything if you want it enough. Remember what I taught you? Reach out and you'll find what you need.*

So once again, she placed the clarinet to her lips. But this time, instead of concentrating on which note followed which, she relaxed into the music, giving rein to the emotions of the last few hours. Instead of stifling them, she allowed her feelings to become an integral part of the music.

Her playing had a depth and sensitivity that even her mother would have had difficulty finding fault with, and Jenna knew she was playing as she'd never played in her life before — nor, she suspected, would she ever play so well again. The beautiful, melodic sounds seemed to come from her soul.

As she played, she was unaware of the tears that flowed unchecked down her cheeks and trickled down her neck. When she reached the end of the piece and put the instrument down across its case, they continued to fall. Tears of grief; of being abandoned; of so many wasted years. But most of her tears were for the young schoolgirl at the concert, sick with disappointment at the sight of an empty chair.

'Why didn't you come that night?' she demanded of the empty shadows. 'Why, when it was obvious from your letter that you intended to? Was Luke right after all? Mum wouldn't do a dreadful thing like that . . . would she? How could she do something so cruel?'

You know the answer to that. This time; it was not her father's voice inside her head, but a small, cruel one of her own.

Because she never loved you, that's how. You heard what she said the day James fell off his bike. You saw the way she looked at you. Whatever you did, it would never make her love you. All her love was for James. There was nothing left for you, not even at the end. No matter how well you cared for her, it was James who'd make her light up with pleasure when he came to visit and made her eyes fill with tears that last, awful week when he stopped coming.

But even that didn't stop her loving him — whereas all you did, giving up your flat, your job, it was all for nothing. Oh yes, she appreciated what you had done. But at the end, she still couldn't love you.

'But I didn't do it for that reason!'

Jenna cried aloud, sinking down onto the bale of hay.

No? the voice inside her head sneered. *Then why? Out of pity? Not out of love, surely? Not after what she did to you. Why, she didn't even love you enough to leave you a share in the place that had been your home.*

Jenna couldn't argue any more. Huge shuddering sobs shook her body and left her so weak she would have collapsed on the cold floor of the barn but for a strong pair of arms that reached out to encircle her.

In her frenzy of weeping, she hadn't noticed Luke hobbling into the barn and lowering himself painfully on to the hay bale beside her.

'Jenna. Jenna,' he whispered, his breath fanning the top of her head as he held her close into his chest. 'Don't cry like that. You'll make yourself ill.'

But her tears, now started, had gained a momentum of their own, just as a snowball rolling down a hill gathers more snow. They began as the tears she should have shed on the night of the concert, but didn't. Then they were the tears she should have shed at her father's funeral but hadn't. Next they were the tears she didn't cry at her mother's funeral — and, finally, they were the tears for a young child whose mother couldn't love her.

She was crying them all now, all at once, and she didn't think they would ever stop.

Luke held her close and made no further attempt to stop her.

Eventually, though, they began to subside, although she still clung to Luke for support.

'I-I've been thinking about . . . what you said,' she murmured, her voice coming in gulps as she struggled to regain control. 'About why she would do what she did.'

Luke shrugged. 'I dare say she had her reasons,' he said. 'Probably thought she was doing what was best for you.'

'She never loved me, you know.' Jenna's voice was so low that he had to bend his head closer in order to hear her.

'Of course she did. Why on earth wouldn't she?'

Jenna felt her throat tighten as tears threatened again. 'Because I'm not James — my brother.' Bitterly, she recited her mother's words aloud. '"James is clever and gifted. Never clumsy, awkward or tactless. He never loses anything, including his temper. He's charming. He's so good-looking.' In short — he's everything that I'm not.'

'What total nonsense!'

'It's not,' she protested. 'Do you know how much my mother loved me, Luke?'

'How can I answer that?'

'Then I'll tell you.' Jenna's voice was harsh as all the anger, all the hurt and resentment she'd denied and bitten back for so long came pouring out. 'She loved me so much, she didn't even leave me a share in her house. Our family home. She left that to my brother. Do

135

you know why?'

Luke shook his head, but Jenna wasn't waiting for any response. She was going to tell him anyway as her tears now gave way to anger.

'Because she felt Dad treated James unfairly by leaving me Brackwith — or at least a share in it. She thought she'd even things out by leaving him the cottage. But I swear to you I didn't know about Brackwith. I assumed it had been sold when they split up.'

'You didn't know?' Luke stared at her, as if trying to decide whether or not to believe her. 'She had no right to keep that from you. In fact, I can't think how she managed it.'

Jenna shrugged. 'Well, she did,' she answered, sudden exhaustion echoing in her voice. 'And do you know the really funny thing? I hadn't even realised, until now, that she didn't love me. I'd been kidding myself all these years. I suppose I always hoped the next thing I did that pleased her would do it.

'But now, I can see that would never

happen, no matter what I did. I could never be what she wanted me to be.'

'Which was?'

'A female version of James — bright, intelligent, musically gifted, graceful, beautiful. Must I go on? Easier to say that James is everything I am not.'

'But you *are* bright and intelligent — and as for being musically talented, well, I'm no music critic but I heard you playing just now and ... ' He searched for the right words. 'Well, hearing that made the hairs stand up on the back of my neck, it was that good. And if that's not musical talent, I don't know what is.'

'That was a one-off,' Jenna muttered brokenly. 'I've never played like that before — nor ever will again. And even that is nowhere near James's league. You know he's studying at the Royal College of Music, don't you? Nor am I in the same league academically. Oh, I scraped a reasonable degree after a great deal of hard work whereas he saunters through everything.'

'Poor you, growing up in your little brother's shadow. Still, I imagine that you managed to make it suitably uncomfortable for him at times.'

Jenna frowned as she detected a lightening in the tone of his voice. Was he teasing her? She gave him a cold stare but couldn't sustain it. She could never stay angry for long. James had learned from an early age that the easiest way to deflect her anger was to appeal to her sense of the ridiculous and make her laugh. Luke obviously realised this, too.

'You're right.' She gave in and laughed. 'Poor James. I'm afraid I made his life a misery at times, the things I used to make him do, particularly when it came to acting in my plays — or trying to keep up with me in a bike race. I was such a bossy boots. But I had to maintain some advantage over him. After all, I was the one standing behind the door when the good fairy was handing out the gifts.'

Luke shook his head, smiling at her.

'You wouldn't be fishing for compliments, would you?' he challenged. 'I'd have said false modesty wasn't your way at all.'

'Of course not. How could you say that?'

'Well — ' Luke reached for her hand and began counting off on her fingers, 'Let me see, I've already said you're bright, intelligent and musically talented. It remains for me to tell you that you have a natural grace that would arouse envy in any supermodel and, of course, you're stunningly beautiful.'

Jenna flushed. 'I don't think that's funny,' she snapped. She tried to pull her hand away, but Luke held it fast.

'You don't know, do you?' He shook his head in amazement. 'You really don't know.'

'Know what?' Jenna was irritable now that her lighter mood had been crushed again so easily.

'You have no idea how very beautiful you are, do you?' Luke murmured as he traced a fingertip, gentle as a feather, across her cheekbone towards her parted lips.

'But I'm *not* — ' Jenna started to protest. He silenced her by increasing the pressure of his finger on her lips.

'Your hair is the colour of burnished copper, your skin looks and feels like cream satin and those freckles on your nose . . . ' he pulled her closer until her face was so close to his that she could feel the warmth of his breath on her face.

'Yes?' She noticed that his eyes weren't light blue at all, as she'd first thought, but a deep grey flecked with sapphire, which gave them the iridescence of a dragonfly's wing.

'Those freckles on your nose are just made for kissing,' he said, his voice hoarse as he lowered his head and kissed her gently on the bridge of her nose.

His lips felt cool against her skin, yet the sensation sent a shockwave through her as if she'd received a jolt of electricity, causing her to catch her breath and pull back from him. As soon as she did, however, she regretted it. Their faces were a few inches apart, yet neither moved. Her eyes were on a level with his mouth and she was surprised to realise that his breathing was as uneven as hers. She wondered what it would be like to feel his lips on hers, and unconsciously she moistened her lips with her tongue.

She heard his sharp intake of breath and, for one awful moment, thought he was going to pull away. She wouldn't let that happen. She raised her head, her eyes meeting his, her lips a fraction of an inch away from his. She saw the flicker of doubt in his eyes silenced by the answer in hers. It was the slightest of movements, the smallest of distances that brought his mouth down on hers and yet, to Jenna it felt as if she'd taken a giant leap into a new world.

She'd been kissed many times, but she'd never experienced anything like the effect that Luke's kiss was having on her. It was gentle at first, then more urgent and demanding as he responded to Jenna's eagerness.

She trailed her fingertips across the back of his neck, thrilling in his little groan of pleasure as she did so. Luke had told her she was beautiful — and although she didn't believe him, just at that moment, as she lost all her inhibitions in his kiss, she felt that she was. Joy surged up in her like a song as she drew her fingers through his hair. For the first time in her life, she felt her body come alive, truly alive, and she delighted in it.

She'd always been self-conscious. She was too tall, too thin, hence Stick Insect, James's nickname for her. Her red hair was an embarrassment, her freckles even more so. But in that moment, she could see herself through Luke's eyes and believe the message of his kisses.

Nobody had ever described her hair colour as 'burnished copper' before. She was more used to hearing it likened to carrots. She tried to tell herself it was just his clever use of words; that being a novelist, he had a gift with words. But still they pleased her, and she knew she'd been seduced by his words as much as by his actions.

But, oh, those actions! She felt as if her bones were dissolving as he traced feather-soft fingertips across her face and down her throat, leaving tingles of pleasure wherever they touched. He pushed back her open-necked blouse, exposing her bare shoulder.

'You even have freckles across your shoulders,' he said in a voice thickened with emotion. 'Angel's Dust, I've heard them called. I want to kiss every single one.' He bent his head and began, with tantalising gentleness, to kiss the line of her shoulder blade.

'Tell me,' he said, pulling back, his gaze resting on the top button on her blouse. 'Have the angels been scattering their dust all over your body?'

'That's for me to know and you to find out.' She smiled, arching her body towards him, inviting him to share her newfound delight in it.

He muttered something under his breath and pressed her to him so hard that she felt the roughness of his sweater against her exposed skin. She could feel his heart beating as wildly as hers as he bent to kiss her shoulders again, sending her senses reeling so that she longed to tear her clothes off — his too — aching for the pleasure of his bare skin against hers.

Then, with a shattering abruptness, he pulled away from her. She whimpered a protest which soon changed to concern.

'Luke, I'm so sorry.' She saw he was bent double with pain. 'That was stupid of me. I shouldn't have — '

As if on cue, they heard the shrill of the telephone inside the house.

'I'll go.' She jumped up. 'You stay there for a while until you're feeling better.'

'For God's sake, woman!' He swore at the pain as he reached for his crutches. 'I'm not an invalid. I'm quite capable of answering my own phone.'

Jenna stared after him, unable to believe what had just happened. She'd just thrown herself at a married man — the very same man whom she'd spent the last seven years of her life hating with a passion.

How could she have behaved like that? What was happening to her?

9

Jenna sat without moving for so long after Luke left that the small red hen was joined by two others, persuaded by Jenna's stillness that she was no threat to them. They clucked and strutted at her feet, engrossed in their intricate ritual and as indifferent to her as she was to them, until suddenly she stood up. Then with startled squawks they half-flew, half-ran in slaloms of panic in front of her as she left the barn.

The snow, which had just started as she entered the barn, had been falling ever since. How long ago was that? It was now twelve-thirty and although she hadn't checked her watch as she came out of the house, she guessed it must have been about half past eleven.

Just one hour. That such a change could happen in a short time, a blanket of snow transforming everyday things into the extraordinary, was one of the things she'd loved about snowstorms as a child. But now came the renewed awful realisation that one of those extraordinary objects was her car — her sole means of escape from this unbearable situation.

The snow pattered down in large, ragged flakes. Across the yard ran the strange trail of prints left in the snow by Luke and his crutches. Those near the back door showed the prints going in several directions which suggested that maybe Luke had got to the door, turned and taken a few steps back towards the barn before changing his mind and going into the house. If that was so, she was glad he'd not returned to the barn. There was no way she could have faced him again.

The only thing she'd decided as she sat in the semi-darkness in the barn was that she should get away from Brackwith — and Luke — before she awoke any more painful old memories.

Or, Heaven forbid, before she got

herself involved with a married man. She felt a swift uprush of shame at the memory of the way in which Luke had kissed her, not to mention the enthusiastic way in which she'd responded. What had she been thinking of?

She forced herself to walk normally through the house, refusing to give in to the temptation to tiptoe as she went up to the room where she had slept the night before. Even so, she was careful not to make unnecessary noise. All she wanted was to get away as quickly and quietly as possible with no recriminations or embarrassment; no apologies or explanations.

She hunted in her overnight bag for her writing things, so anxious to avoid Luke that she resolved to take the easy way out and leave a note rather than face him. So what if he thought her a coward? What harm was being branded a coward, compared to some of the other things he must think of her?

And why should she care what he thought of her, anyway?

She sat down at the old pine table by the window, chewing the end of her pen as she tried in vain to find the right words.

'Jenna?'

The sound of his voice, unexpectedly close behind her, made her jump so violently that the pen scored a jagged line across the paper.

'For Heaven's sake!' Shock made her voice sharper than she'd intended. 'Don't you have the courtesy to knock? How dare you creep up on me like that!'

'Your door was open. I did knock, but you were so engrossed you didn't hear me. As for creeping up on you, that's a bit difficult for a man on crutches, wouldn't you say? However, if I startled you, I'm sorry. Would you like me to go out of the room and start again?'

As he spoke, Jenna could see the beginnings of a smile, as if he was about to start teasing her again. But she ignored it and hung on to her anger. It was the only way she was going to get out of the situation without too much damage to her pride.

'That won't be necessary.' She forced her voice to remain cool; her eyes, as they looked into his, steady. 'I was writing you a note, but now you're here, I can tell you in person.'

'Tell me that?'

'I'm leaving. Now.'

Luke peered out of the window. 'I'm afraid you're not going anywhere. Have you seen it out there? The wind's getting up and it's a near whiteout. You'd be crazy to even think of it.

Jenna shrugged. 'I've driven in snow before,' she said with a confidence she didn't feel but would never admit to faking. 'I'll take it steady. It won't be a problem.'

'Won't be a problem? For Heaven's sake, woman, of course it will! You've lived up here. Surely you remember how bad things can get in weather like this?'

'Nevertheless, I'm going,' she said as

her chin came up, her mouth set in a hard line and her eyes darkened. It was a gesture that anyone who knew her would recognise as Jenna about to dig her heels in, hard.

Luke's eyes locked on hers and they glared at each other like two cats, each willing the other to back down.

Luke was the first to look away.

'Jenna . . . ' He sighed heavily. 'If it's about what happened in the barn just now — '

'Of course it's not.' Jenna turned away, put her overnight bag on the bed and began placing things into it with meticulous concentration.

'Look, I'm sorry.' He moved to take the bag from her, but she backed away like a startled colt. 'Please stay. I promise I won't lay a finger on you again.' He sighed again. 'Look, what happened back there . . . Can't you simply forget it? I promise you I have.'

She turned away and looked out at the driving snow. So, he'd forgotten about it, had he? He could dismiss what had happened between them so lightly?

'Jenna, listen to me, please. We must talk.'

She turned to face him. 'I don't think there's anything to talk about, do you?' she retorted. 'Like you, I've forgotten it happened. It meant nothing.'

'I didn't mean that,' he countered. Did she imagine the edge to his voice, as if he was having difficulty concealing his contempt? 'I meant,' he went on, speaking the words slowly and carefully as if to a child, 'that we must talk about Brackwith.'

'Oh.' To her dismay, she felt her cheeks begin to burn. What was the matter with her today? Why was she behaving like a twelve-year-old?

'Well?' He ignored her embarrassment. 'Have you given it any thought?'

'Is this the time to be discussing it?' She picked up her bag and resisted the impulse to break into a run as she headed for the door. 'I'll get my solicitor to speak to yours as soon as I get back. Now, I must go, before the weather sets in, so if you'll excuse me — '

'You can't. You can't go.' The desperation in his voice was so unexpected that she stopped and turned back, her eyes mirroring her surprise.

'I'd really like you to stay. I don't want to be on my own.'

'But surely your wife — '

'I don't have a wife. That was something I made up so that I could leave hospital.'

For one crazy moment, Jenna felt a wild surge of — what? Was it hope that made her heart suddenly beat faster?

Yet what difference did it make to her whether he was married or not? He was still Luke Grantley, the man who'd left her father on a mountain to die.

'So will you stay? Please.'

'I'm sorry,' she said crisply, although the little pause before the word 'please' had almost wriggled under her defences. 'I've got to go, now. Besides, you were keen enough to send me packing last night.'

There was a long, tense silence between them and Jenna felt a surge of triumph as, for the moment at least, she appeared to be winning this latest battle of wills. She didn't know Luke very well but she was convinced that the man who last night told her to go, insisting he was capable of looking after himself, was the real Luke Grantley. This . . . this nonsense about him not wanting to be on his own was no more than a trick to persuade her to stay.

No, she'd take her chance with the weather; she felt safer with the blizzard than she did at Brackwith with its secrets, its ghosts — and Luke.

She picked up her bag and car keys and headed for the door. He stood aside to let her pass and she started to walk along the landing towards the stairs.

'Jenna.' He called after her, his voice urgent. 'For God's sake, don't go. I really don't want to be on my own. These damned nightmares.'

'Nightmares?' She turned unwillingly and went back into the room where he stood by the window, staring out at the gathering storm. His face was impassive, but his expression was that of a man staring, not at the coming snowstorm, but over the edge of an abyss.

'Well?' Her voice was gentler.

'Since the accident,' he said, 'I've had flashbacks. Most of us get that horrible dream at one time or another. You know, the one where you think you're falling? Well, in my case it was no dream, it was for real. I was falling. It comes back some nights, usually in the small hours of the morning and I'm falling again.

'I feel every thud and jolt; I hear every crunch and groan; I feel the breath being sucked out of my body, all the way down, just like before. Only this time . . . I'm wide awake when I finally hit the bottom.'

Jenna felt a wave of sympathy towards him, as she recognised the truth and what it must have cost him to tell it.

'Have you told anybody? Don't the sleeping tablets help?'

He shook his head. 'I'll cope. But Sister Martin was right, you know. I would prefer not to be up here on my own at the moment. So, will you stay . . . please?'

Once again, there was the tiny hesitation before the word 'please'. It made her realise how much this proud, independent man must hate having to ask anything of anyone. Least of all her. Fury began to burn inside her at the cruel accident that had brought him to this.

'Was it worth it?' The bitter words poured out before she could stop them. 'Your accident; the nightmares. What was it all for? An adrenaline rush you can't get anywhere else? One more notch on your belt? One more summit bagged? Or the buzz of pushing yourself to the limit and peering over the edge, the way my father used to? Only this time, Luke, you didn't peer over the edge, did you? This time, you fell over the edge. So, I repeat — was it worth it?'

She glared at him, green eyes blazing. He shrugged and would have turned away but she grabbed his arm, almost causing him to overbalance.

'Go on, tell me.' She steadied him, then pointed to his crutches. 'Tell me it was worth it.'

'It was the only place I could get any peace that day,' he snapped. 'You wouldn't — '

He stopped in mid-sentence and stared at her as if trying to make up his mind about something. She had an uneasy feeling she was about to be told something she'd prefer not to know.

'You wouldn't understand,' he muttered eventually.

'I might,' she said, conscious of the risk she was taking.

'Maybe I will tell you.' He gave her a slow, speculative look, 'You are, after all, Lynda Manning's daughter, as your outburst has just reminded me. But not now. Right now I'm more concerned with whether or not you're going to stay.'

'You still want me to stay, even after my — what did you call it? — my outburst? I'm not going to apologise for what I said, if that's what you're hoping.'

Before he could answer, a furious gust of wind slapped handfuls of snow against the windows. Luke turned. Jenna, too, looked at the raging storm which had changed the pretty Christmas-card scene outside into something far more sinister.

Then she looked back towards the comfort and safety — even if she was only using the word in its physical sense — of the house. She thought of the long, uneven track, with its deep ruts and unexpected cambers, hazardous even in ideal conditions.

But against that, she recalled what had happened between them in the barn earlier.

She thought, too, of what she wished had happened, how sorry she'd been when he'd pulled away — and that was when she'd thought he was married; that it was loyalty to his wife that had made him turn from her.

Now, she knew differently. Now she knew that, as far as he was concerned, it had been nothing to him. Just a moment of madness; easily forgotten. One thing she knew for sure. She had nothing to fear from Luke trying to kiss her again.

Was he lying about the nightmares? She held his gaze. The hesitant vulnerability that had been there when he'd first asked her to stay was long gone, chased away by her taunts about the futility of risking everything for a mountain. What was it about this man that brought out the worst in her?

It had been a terrible thing to say to someone who was still struggling to come to terms with a disabling accident. How could she have done it? She was ashamed of herself and wished she could have taken back every cruel word.

'I'm sorry.' She pushed her hand through her hair, her eyes brimming with remorse. 'I'm so sorry, Luke. I shouldn't have said that. Mum always used to say I have all the tact of an elephant blundering about in a rose garden. Please forgive me.'

Luke gave her a long, appraising look. 'Your mother was wrong about many things,' he said eventually. 'She was wrong about John, about me, but, most of all, Jenna, I suspect she was wrong about you. Was I wrong, too?'

Once again, the tension that had crackled between them in the barn was suddenly, inexplicably back and the safe, comfortable room didn't feel safe any more.

Then Luke laughed. A sudden, unexpected sound.

'Okay.' He waved one of his crutches in a gesture of surrender. 'Look, I've apologised. You've apologised. What do you say we declare a truce and see what we can find for lunch? I don't know about you, but I'm starving. I only had crumbs for breakfast and that was ages ago.'

Jenna stared at him, trying to adjust to his sudden change of mood. What game was he playing now? She gave a mental shrug and, after a moment, followed him downstairs into the kitchen. If that was the way he wanted to play it, it made a sort of sense. She'd agreed to stay, and things would be easier for them both if they declared a truce, however temporary.

'Crumbs, eh?' She gave a forced laugh as she tried to echo his lighter mood. 'You call that mountain of toast you ploughed through earlier 'crumbs'? I hope your freezer is well stocked. It looks as if keeping you fed is a full-time job.'

'Then you'll take it?' he asked. 'The pay is lousy but working conditions are excellent, not to mention the job satisfaction.'

'I'll take it,' she said. 'At least until

the weather clears.'

Luke opened the fridge and peered inside. 'We have eggs, tomatoes, mushrooms and bacon. And, to prove I'm not a complete inadequate, I can do you a first class fry-up with that lot, if you fancy it.'

Jenna wrinkled her nose. 'Not really — but I can offer a mushroom and bacon omelette with a tomato salad. How does that sound?'

'Hmmm. Not so good, but probably a lot healthier. So, what can I do to help?'

'You can sit there and take the weight off your legs. Sister Martin said plenty of rest, remember?'

'I'm still capable of chopping bacon or whatever,' he growled.

★　★　★

They worked together to prepare the meal. At first, Jenna had to force herself to keep the conversation between them light and easy, but before long she realised she was no longer having to try. Instead, it felt as if they were a couple of old friends who were comfortable in each other's company.

She told him a little about her job and her university days. He told tales of his student days and they swapped horror stories of student parties, grinding poverty and deadline crises, each topping the last in the scale of awfulness.

Then, as they ate, he described his recent round of TV chat shows to promote his latest book and she laughed, protesting at some of his more outrageous stories.

'Please don't,' she begged, wiping her eyes with her napkin. 'I don't believe a word of it anyway, and I'm going to choke if you make me laugh any more. You said you were planning a new book. How's it coming along?'

'Stalled at the moment. But I'll have to get back to it soon otherwise I'll have one very unhappy publisher breathing down my neck.'

He reached to help himself to the last of the bread rolls, remembering in time to offer it to Jenna.

'I couldn't eat another thing,' she said regretfully. 'How can anyone eat as much as you do and stay so slim?'

'It's because I lead such an active life,' he said confidently, then paused as a shadow crossed his face. 'Or rather, I used to,' he corrected himself.

Jenna clapped her hand to her mouth. When, oh when would she learn to think before she spoke?

'I've done it again, haven't I? Me and my big mouth. I am so sorry, Luke.'

10

'For Heaven's sake.' He pushed his plate to one side and grasped her hand. 'I think I liked you better when you were beating me up about being clumsy enough to fall off a mountain. Will you stop tiptoeing around me as if you're walking on eggshells? I can't stand it.'

'I'm sorry.'

'And you can stop apologising, too.'

'Right.' She took a deep, steadying breath as she tried to recapture their previous easygoing banter. 'If that's the way you want it. Although don't say you haven't been warned if I start criticising the way you've had your hair cut, or your taste in curtains. You can have as many broken eggshells as you wish. On one condition.'

'Which is?'

'That you let go of my hand before you either cut off the circulation or break one of my fingers — always assuming you haven't already done so, of course.'

'Oh — I'm so sorry.' He released her hand at once. 'I had no idea I was — '

'Oh, yes — and there's one more condition. That you stop apologising and all,' she said in a reasonable imitation of his faint, but unmistakable Yorkshire accent.

Luke roared with laughter. 'You sounded so much like your father,' he said, 'That's exactly how he used to tease me. You're almost as good a mimic, too.'

The laughter between them died as if it was canned studio laughter cut off by the flick of a switch.

'Is — is there something around here to read?' Jenna tried to steer the conversation to safer ground. She took the empty plates to the sink, where she began splashing water over them.

'I've never read any of your books, although James has read every single one and is a huge fan. In fact, if he were here now, he'd probably have you chained to your desk, getting on with the next one.' She squirted far too much washing-up liquid in the bowl and tutted with annoyance as the bubbles in the bowl swelled like a giant puffball.

'So which do you recommend I try first? Do you have a favourite? Which —?'

'Jenna. This won't do and you know it.' His voice was quiet, his words few — a marked contrast to her own frantic babble. 'We've got to talk about him properly, sooner or later.'

'I'd prefer not to.' She concentrated fiercely on scooping out bubbles from the bowl.

'John was — indeed, still is — a central part of my life,' he went on. 'And, I suspect, of yours too. He's what we have in common — him and Brackwith, of course. It's not possible to spend any time together and not talk about him. Or, if not him, then at least let's talk about Brackwith and my plans for it.'

She whirled round, suds dripping from her hands to the floor. 'Of course — your plans for Brackwith. Yes, why don't we talk about them? Why don't you tell me how you're planning to turn this place into a fancy hotel, full of tourists in four-wheel drives and designer gear? And while you're about it, why not tell me how you can bear to look at yourself in the mirror each morning? If you knew my father as well as you claim, you must surely know how he'd have hated such a thing.'

'How would you know what your father would or wouldn't have hated?'

It was there again. The antagonism that flared between them every time John's name was mentioned. He was the one thing they had in common, yet also their main cause of conflict. Luke resented her because of the way she'd hurt her father, while she found it hard to believe she was sitting here with the man she still blamed for her father's death, laughing with him, eating with him — and, worst of all, kissing him.

It was, surely, the worst kind of betrayal.

If she could have turned the clock back, it would have been to the moment in Mr Bennington's office when she'd first learned about her share in Brackwith. Then she'd have taken everyone's advice and sold her interest in the farmhouse without ever coming back here.

But she hadn't — so she was stuck with the situation, just as Luke was stuck with her. But there was no way she was going to sit back and watch as Brackwith was 'restored' and turned into the kind of over-prettified, over-priced country hotel her father disliked so much without doing something, anything, to stop it. She owed him that much.

'I know Dad would have hated to see Brackwith turned into a smart hotel, complete with thick pile carpets, window boxes and hanging baskets,' she said. 'Maybe that's why he left half to me, knowing I'd stop you. So, tell me about your plans and, whilst you're about it, tell me where I fit in. Chambermaid? Scullery maid?'

'Oh, definitely the scullery maid.' He reached across and before she could anticipate what he was about to do, scooped a handful of soap bubbles from the bowl and deposited them on the end of her nose. 'Yes, a scullery maid,' he repeated, with an infuriating grin. 'I'm afraid you're much too forward to be considered for the chambermaid's job.'

'But — ' Jenna raised her hand to wipe the bubbles away but again he was too quick for her. He held her wrist, stopping her hand from reaching her face.

'Poor Jenna,' he said with a smile. 'I shouldn't tease you, not about something as important as this. But it's hard to resist because that's another way in which you're so like John. You've the same fiery temper and like him are always ready to rise to the bait.'

She pushed his hand away with an

impatient gesture and wiped the soap from her nose. 'What are you talking about? Is this your latest game, talking in riddles? Well, I'm sorry to be a spoilsport but I'm not playing.'

'No, I'm the one who's sorry. I won't tease you any more, I promise. Come in to the study. There's something I want to show you.'

* * *

Jenna was puzzled as she followed him along the dark hallway. For a moment she hesitated at the door before going back into the room where she'd spent so many happy hours as a child. Now it aroused a mass of conflicting emotions in her at the thought of how much she'd lost, and the knowledge that things between her and her father could never be put right.

It was too late. Four small but heart-breaking words.

She blinked hard as tears prickled her eyelids. What on earth was happening to her lately? She, who never cried, seemed to be constantly on the brink, if not actually crying. It was as if coming back here had breached a dam that had been holding back her tears for so many years; tears that, once released, now lurked just beneath the surface of her self-control, ready to flow at any moment.

'Well, what do you think?'

Luke's voice was a welcome intrusion and she looked down at the folder he'd placed in her hands.

The John Manning Centre, she read the bold black lettering on the front. 'What is it?'

'It's the plans for what I'd like to do here.'

Jenna was confused by the pages of drawings and closely packed text. She was usually quick to extract the essence of a report from charts and data, but at that moment all she could see was a mass of lines and text; all slightly out of focus.

'What plans?' she asked faintly. 'And for where?'

Luke waved his hand around. 'Right here, of course. Well, not exactly here in the house. I thought we could convert some of the outbuildings. There are several in surprisingly good condition that would make first-rate accommodation blocks.'

'Accommodation blocks?' she echoed, still struggling to work out what he was talking about. 'What for? Are you planning to turn the place into a boarding school?'

'Not exactly, but close.' Luke took the folder from Jenna's hands, pulled out one of the architect's plans and spread it on the desk in front of them.

'Remember I told you how coming here turned my life around? I want to be able to do that for other underprivileged kids. There's enough of them out there, more's the pity. I'd like to turn this into a place where kids come to learn all sorts of things — not only climbing, although that would be a core activity, of course, but everything, from making music to pottery to acting. A whole raft of things, exciting activities that will stretch them in ways they haven't been stretched before.'

'And you're going to call the place after Dad?' Jenna forced herself to concentrate on the positive side of what he said and to ignore the doubts screaming for attention inside her head.

Luke nodded. 'The John Manning Centre. It couldn't be called anything else, could it? Can you think of a more fitting memorial? Far more appropriate than the stuffy portrait of him I saw in my old school when I visited it recently. No — he'd have been tickled pink by this, I know it.'

He pointed to the plans. Jenna thought of the children, many of them boys like Luke had once been, who used to come to Brackwith. Surly and defiant when they first arrived, sparkling with confidence and enthusiasm by the time they left.

'Yes, I think he would,' she admitted reluctantly.

'And you?' He was watching her

intently as he spoke. 'How do you feel about it?'

'I haven't had time to think it through.' she said, choosing her words with care.

'Look,' he said. 'I know this is probably not the right time to say this. Probably shouldn't say it at all, but my offer to buy your share in Brackwith still stands, if that's what's bothering you. You've got to find yourself somewhere to live and if I hadn't made that offer to your mother, she'd have probably left you a share of her house. So, I suppose what I'm trying to say is that I feel partly responsible for the unfair way she treated you and would like to help.'

'But it wasn't unfair.' Jenna was glad that, in one respect, at least, she was able to put Luke right about her mother. 'She was trying to even things up because Dad treated James unfairly by leaving Brackwith — or at least, part of it — to me and not to us both.'

'Unfair?' Luke's brows closed together

in a dark line. 'But he left James the royalties on his most successful books, which would have more than covered it. Surely you knew that?'

Jenna was stunned. 'I didn't. And I'm pretty sure James didn't know that either. He's hopeless at keeping secrets and could never have kept something like that from me.'

Luke shrugged. 'Maybe John changed his mind,' he said. 'Certainly he told me that was what he was planning to do. It was to fund James through music college, I believe. I remember thinking at the time it was unfair on you, but thought it was none of my business. I certainly didn't know you were the other co-owner of Brackwith. I can't believe you didn't know.'

'Believe what you like,' Jenna retorted, rattled by the unexpected turn the conversation had taken. 'Mum never discussed finance with us. I didn't even know I'd been left Brackwith until after she'd died. My solicitor will confirm that, if you don't believe me.'

'Oh, I believe you,' he said. 'Jenna, I'm sorry about some of those things I said about you yesterday, although I still maintain that people who eavesdrop deserve to hear bad things, and what you were doing, deceiving me, was the worst sort of — '

'You've already said that.' Jenna had no wish to have to justify her deception again.

'So I have.' He smiled briefly. 'You know, you have been most unfairly treated,' he went on, his voice gentle as he took her hand. 'Would you let me make up for it in a small way, by buying your share in Brackwith? My offer was a generous one, but I'm willing to increase it by another five thousand pounds.'

Jenna snatched her hand away and resisted the urge to rub at the tingle on her skin where his hand had rested on hers. She raised her chin, her mouth set in a firm line, her eyes darkened. No way she was going to let him feel sorry for her.

'And what happens to your plans for Brackwith if I don't accept your generous offer?'

Luke shrugged and began putting the drawings back in the folder. 'In that case we remain joint owners. Nothing changes.'

She crossed her arms defensively. 'And if that's what I want? For nothing to change? What happens to your plans if I decide I don't want the John Manning Centre to go ahead?'

She flinched from the intensity of Luke's vivid blue gaze and wanted to cry out at the unfairness of it. All she needed was the chance to sort things out in her head before making a decision. She'd had no time to absorb the fact she'd inherited Brackwith before having to adjust to the fact that she shared it with Luke. Now, as she was getting used to that, she was asked to choose whether to share Brackwith with delinquent kids hell-bent on becoming the next generation of mountaineers — or sell out.

But what else was there? Surely she didn't see any future for herself here with Luke? Of course not. For Heaven's sake, she didn't even like the man — did she?

'Look.' His eyes softened as he leaned towards her. 'This is something I'm passionately committed to, and for a moment I felt you were, too. This place could do so much good for so many people. Not just the kids but their families, schools, neighbours, in fact anyone who comes in contact with them. Like ripples from a stone thrown into a pond.

'If coming here works for a small minority, even a minority of one, it will have been worth it. If I can take that single angry child and, as John did for me, channel that anger into positive energy; if, by teaching him to climb I can at the same time teach him to reach inside himself and discover a strength he — '

He stopped. The light died in his eyes. 'Yes, well.' He looked down at his crutches. 'Somebody else will probably be doing that. But that's not the point. This isn't about me.'

It's very much the point, she wanted to scream. To remind him that the urge to climb mountains was a destructive force, not to be fostered in impressionable young people.

She wanted to tell him how her father's obsession — for how else could she describe an activity that drove a man to give up his wife, his family, his home and even, in the end, his life? — had blighted not only her life but other people's lives too, just like Luke's ripples on a pond.

She wanted to say it was precisely *because* she was John Manning's daughter that she couldn't support a venture that would introduce vulnerable young people to the dangerous, addictive sport of climbing.

But how could she say all that to him as she watched his struggle to accept that he would now have to depend on somebody else to make his dream come true?

11

Jenna stood at the window watching one of the hens scratching anxiously at the snow, searching for signs of normality. That was just how she felt — as if everything familiar had been swept away or called into question.

Nothing made sense any more. Luke's plans went against everything she believed in — and yet, for just a minute, she let herself imagine what it would be like to stay here at Brackwith and help put his plans into action.

She looked up at Brackwith Pike. The snow had stopped and the mountain stood in sharp relief against the winter sky, its barren, rocky sides now sculpted into softer contours by the blanket of snow. It was a truly magnificent sight and she experienced a moment of intense pleasure, like sunlight breaking through a cloud.

It was over in a second. But, like the sunlight, the moment left behind a lingering warmth as, for the first time since leaving Brackwith all those years ago, she could look up at a mountain without a shudder of fear and loathing.

She took a deep breath, proud of how steady her voice sounded. 'It sounds great.' She even managed a smile. 'And you're right, of course. Dad would have loved it.'

'Wouldn't he just,' Luke said warmly. 'It was something he'd got going himself on an informal basis, before he — '

'Which of the outbuildings do you have in mind for the accommodation?' she cut in, anxious to stop him completing the sentence. 'And what about the hens? You're going to have to find them an alternative scratching ground if you use the Big Barn, you know.'

'No, I'd like to leave the Barn as it is, as I'm sure you would,' he said. 'John used to tell me about the concerts and parties you held there. You must have some great memories of the place, if only half of the stories he told are true.'

To Jenna's horror, she felt a blush travel up her neck towards her cheeks as her thoughts flew back to a more recent memory of the Big Barn that had nothing to do with her father. Beneath her clothes, she could feel her flesh tingle at the memory of Luke's lips, cool against her fevered skin. She closed her eyes and turned away from him, as if by doing so she could shut out the images her thoughts had conjured up.

The silence was shattered by the phone ringing, and she sent a silent prayer of thanks to whoever had diverted Luke's attention from her and her burning cheeks.

Her relief was short-lived, however. He picked it up, listened for a second, and then a teasing grin lit his face.

'She is indeed. In fact, she's right here. Would you like to speak to her?' He covered the mouthpiece with his hand and beckoned her towards him. 'It's the man who phoned earlier when we were in the barn. I told him you were . . . ' He hesitated, and from the laughter in his eyes, appeared to be relishing her discomfort, ' . . . indisposed.'

'James? What's wrong?' James was the only person she had given the number for Brackwith.

'It's not James. It's me. Steven. James gave me your number. Jenna, are you all right?'

'Of course I am.' She forced a light laugh. 'Why do you ask?'

'You sound a bit odd, that's all. And when I phoned earlier the chap who answered said — well, I thought he meant you were ill. I've been going out my mind with worry. Are you? If so, I can come and get you. I can be with you in less than five hours.'

'There's no need, I promise, Steven. And I'm sorry you've been worried.' She glared at Luke, who grinned and gave her a what-have-I-done-now? look.

'I'm fine, really I am. Never better. I wasn't around when you phoned earlier because . . . I was outside. I — I went for a walk.'

Luke raised his eyebrows and put his hands together in a silent mockery of applause.

'Excuse me a moment,' she murmured to Steven before putting her hand over the phone and rounding on Luke. 'Would you mind if I took this call somewhere more private?'

He shrugged, unmoved by the anger in her eyes or the ice in her voice. 'No need. I'm out of here anyway.' He gave one last infuriating grin and swung out of the room on his crutches.

'What's wrong?' she asked, as the door closed behind Luke.

'Nothing's wrong,' Steven said hastily. 'I don't want to pressure you, but someone else is about to be offered that job I told you about, unless you can get your application in within two days. What do you think?'

Jenna was stunned. The problem of

whether to move to London seemed a million miles away.

'Steven — I — I don't know. I'm not sure I — '

'You don't have to decide anything now, but what have you got to lose by having a go for it anyway? You can make your mind up if, or when, they offer you the job. After all, you never know. You might love it.'

Jenna looked out of the window. She saw one solitary bird — she thought maybe it was a buzzard — wheeling about, its huge wings glinting in the late afternoon light. It appeared to be the only living thing in that huge landscape. Then she thought of crowded commuter trains; of queues for cash machines, taxis and pre-packed sandwiches.

She saw the empty track that led back towards Ambleside and thought of pavements packed with lunchtime shoppers; of escalators like assembly lines carrying an endless stream of people to be swallowed up by the dark, airless tunnels of the Underground.

'I'm sorry,' she said. 'I have thought about it, Steven, and my answer has to be no, I'm afraid. Thank you so much for the offer but the job, London and everything — but it's not for me.'

The silence at the other end of the line went on for so long that she began to think they'd been cut off.

'Steven? Are you still there?'

'I'm still here,' he said at last. 'I'm sorry I pushed things. Perhaps if I hadn't — '

'My answer would still have been the same,' she said gently. 'It may have taken a little longer, that's all.'

'But we can still see each other at weekends, things like that . . . can't we?'

It had been a strange roller-coaster of a day. She had no idea what her future would be, still less what she wanted it to be. But the one thing, the only thing she knew for sure, was that her future did not include Steven — at least, not in the way in which he'd like to be included. She owed it to him to tell him so, quickly and honestly.

'Steven, I'm so sorry,' she said. 'I hope we can still see each other, but only as friends. We can never be more, although I wish we could, for you're a dear, kind person and you deserve better — ' She swallowed. This was harder than she could have anticipated. 'Better than me.'

This time she made no attempt to break the silence. Apart from telling him again how sorry she was, there was nothing more she could say.

'Well,' he said at last. 'At least now I know how things stand between us, or, I suppose, don't stand would be more accurate. But I meant it when I said I'd like us to stay in touch. If things don't work out up there and you need a friend — well, you know how to get hold of me.'

The line went dead. She stared down at the phone now whirring quietly to itself in her hand.

She replaced the receiver and went down to the kitchen where Luke was making himself a sandwich.

'Want one?' he asked. 'I do a really good — '

'No thanks. I'm not hungry.'

His smile faded at the bleak expression on her face.

'Bad news?' he asked.

'In a way.'

'Want to talk about it?'

'No.' She was in no mood for talking and Luke made no attempt to draw her out. He finished making the sandwiches and put them on a tray.

'I'm all in,' he said, and looked it. There were rings of weariness under his eyes and his bruises stood out more livid than ever against his too-pale skin. 'I think if you don't mind, I'll have this in my room. I'll see you in the morning.'

She carried the tray in for him, checked that he had everything he needed, then went back to the kitchen, grateful for some much-needed solitude.

★ ★ ★

Sleep did not come as easily to Jenna that night as it had done the night before, despite her tiredness. As she lay down, she found that although her body was ready for sleep, her mind was racing away like a runaway train, going over and over what she'd said and done during that long, strange day.

She was still feeling the effects of her restless night as she went into the kitchen the next morning, rubbing her eyes against the strong morning sunlight that poured through the window. She was surprised to find Luke already there, breakfast well under way.

'I overslept.' She took the toast he offered with a smile of thanks. 'I'm sorry.'

'Don't be.' He shrugged. 'You look as if you could do with another couple of hours. Didn't you sleep well?'

Jenna shook her head as she bit into the toast, the sharp taste of the marmalade clean on her tongue. 'Too many things going round my head. Yesterday was all a bit much to take in.

Anyway, what about you? You looked absolutely all-in last night. Were — '
She hesitated, then went on, 'Were you all right?'

'All right?' He paused in the act of spreading his toast, his upraised knife golden-capped with butter. 'In what way?'

'Your nightmares, of course.' Her eyes widened with pretended innocence, as she savoured the moment. 'That was why you asked me to stay last night, wasn't it?'

He stared at her but did not answer.

'So, come on,' she urged. 'You didn't fool me for a moment. Nightmares, indeed! What was the real reason? I was going to have this out with you yesterday, but you looked as dead beat as I felt, so I let you off. Come on then, why were you really so keen for me to stay?'

'All right,' he said. 'But don't blame me if you don't like it. It was corny, but it was the only way I could think of getting you to stay. You were hell-bent

191

on charging out into the snow, as if the devil himself was at your heels, and I couldn't let you do that. And, as I failed in my appeal to your sense of self-preservation, I thought I'd appeal to your sympathy instead.'

'And now?' she asked, denying him the angry retort he was expecting. 'Am I free to go? Is that what you are telling me?'

'My dear Miss Manning,' he said. 'You always were free to go. I've never in my life kept a woman with me against her will.'

I'll bet you haven't! she thought, whilst her treacherous mind once again slipped back to those moments of madness in the barn and her eyes flitted to the curve of his mouth.

'There's been no further snowfall during the night.' he went on. 'The roads are still bad but it will probably be all right if you take it easy.'

'Well, in that case — ' Jenna scraped her chair back.

'Jenna, sit down . . . please,' he said.

'There's something I'd like to discuss with you, something that I've been going over and over in my mind all night.'

'In between the nightmares, I presume?' she asked, her voice saccharine-sweet.

'Look, I'm sorry. It was corny, but I did it for the best of reasons. And I do get nightmares, or flashbacks I think they call them, although they're nothing I can't handle.

'No, this time, I'm not making any false appeal to your sympathy, but a genuine appeal to your business sense. Whether we like it or not, thanks to John's machinations we are business partners. I've already told you my plans for Brackwith and I accept the fact that, as co-owner, you have the right to veto them. But I hope you won't do that until you've at least read through my detailed proposals and met my architect. I promise there's not a Jacuzzi or a hanging basket in sight.'

'What exactly do you want from me?'

'That you let things go on as they

are, at least until I'm back on my feet and can deal with things properly again. This is the worst time for this damned accident to happen. I've got men from the local council due to make a site inspection tomorrow, and if I have to put them off it could be the middle of the summer before I can get them to come back again.'

'Yes, I can see that, but — '

The rest of her words were lost by a sound which, although outside, caused the cups to rattle on the dresser and the cat to dive for the safety of the laundry basket.

'What on earth — ?' she yelled above the noise of a battered Land Rover being driven at full throttle in a very low gear, making the old engine scream as it belched billows of angry black smoke in protest. The noise rose to a crescendo, then came a blessed silence, broken only by the faint whisper of the cups, still swinging on their hooks.

'That,' Luke's voice was soft as he tried to disturb the silence as little as possible, 'is Sister Martin — your safe but uncomfortable, not to say eardrum-shattering, journey back to Ambleside, if that's what you want.'

Jenna watched a small woman, bundled up in an overlarge bright orange waterproof, jump down from the Land Rover and cross the yard. She'd imagined a large, plump lady, not this small, birdlike person.

And yet, now she'd seen her . . . Jenna grinned to herself. Sister Martin was no twittering sparrow, but perhaps a bantam? One of those fighting bantams, maybe, who would —

'Good morning,' Sister Martin boomed and Jenna marvelled that such a tiny frame could produce such a powerful voice. 'How's the patient today?'

'Well, he's — '

'The patient's well and quite capable of answering for himself,' Luke said as he followed Sister Martin into the kitchen on his crutches.

'Any pain? Sleep well? Appetite back to normal yet?'

'Fine. No problems.' His answers were as brief and staccato as her questions.

'Well now, that's not going to get us very far, Mr Grantley, is it?' she said in a quieter voice. 'Let's try again, shall we? How's the pain? Are you managing to keep it under control?'

'It's nothing I can't handle.'

The feisty district nurse gave him a challenging look, which he returned, one black eyebrow upraised. Jenna decided it would be better if she left them, so she excused herself as Sister Martin asked, 'And are you sleeping any better? No more flashbacks?'

Jenna turned back and looked at Luke, who stared her out for a moment, then grinned. 'No, I'm sleeping like a baby now my wife is here. No more nightmares, no more tossing and turning, no more sleeping pills, even. You see what miracles are wrought by the presence of such a good woman to soothe the fevered brow, Sister?'

What game was he playing now?

Jenna stared at him, then remembered. Of course — the site meeting. If Sister Martin found out that she was not Mrs Grantley and was about to leave, she'd have him back in hospital before Jenna was even halfway to Ambleside.

Jenna forced a smile. 'Yes, I'm very good at brow-soothing,' she said quietly. 'Now, if you'll excuse me, I have things to do. I'll see you before you go, Sister?'

She escaped to her room, unable to believe what she'd done. Two days ago, she'd hated Luke Grantley, believing him responsible for her father's death. She'd have done anything to hurt him. Indeed, the opportunity for doing him harm was the main reason behind her original decision to stay.

Yet now, when she had the opportunity to deal him and his precious project a severe blow, she'd backed him up. Why? Why had she done that?

Her entire belief system had been turned upside down, that was why. She twisted her mother's wedding ring, which she wore on her right hand, round and round as she tried to sort out her contradictory thoughts towards the man she'd hated for the last seven years.

At first she'd felt pity for him because of his accident, and admiration for the way he faced it; then she had found to her great surprise, as she got to know him, that she had begun to like him as a person.

But did she really trust him? There was still something about him that made a small voice inside her head whisper, *Danger! Be careful!*

12

She twisted the ring, her fingers working busily, nervously, as if the action might somehow untangle the turmoil raging around inside her head. She shrugged, removed the ring and placed it on the ring finger of her left hand. If she was going to play along with Luke's game, she might as well make her part convincing. She put her doubts aside for the moment, squared her shoulders and went back downstairs.

Luke's face told its own grim story. Sister Martin's examination had obviously caused him a lot of pain and there was a spot of blood on his lower lip where he'd bitten it. His bruises stood out, more lurid than ever, against his ashen face and his eyes burned with such intensity that, for a moment, the mature, self-confident man was stripped away and she saw in them the hell-bent angry teenager he'd once been.

What was it her mother used to say about her father? 'John's a really easy-going person,' she'd say, 'as long as everything's going his way.' Well, by the set of Luke's mouth and the scarcely-contained anger that lit his eyes, it looked as if things were definitely not going his way at the moment. He had, she reckoned, met his match in the diminutive Sister Martin.

'What's wrong?' She looked from Luke's angry eyes to the calm, but determined expression on Sister Martin's face. It was the expression she doubtless used to convince reluctant children to roll up their sleeves for an injection, that plainly said: *I'm immune to tantrums. Nothing you can say or do will make any difference.*

'I've told Mr Grantley I want him back in hospital right away. I'm not happy with these spasms he keeps getting — '

'And I told you, I tripped over the cat,' Luke hissed, sounding like a man very near the end of his patience.

'Have you had these spasms before?' the nurse asked.

'No,' said Luke then glared at Jenna as she cut across him.

'Yes. He's had three to my knowledge in the last few days. I'm sorry, Luke, but there's no point ignoring them.'

'Quite,' Sister Martin said. 'I'm glad one of you has some sense at least. Look at you, man. You're the colour of cold porridge and as for your blood pressure — not good. Not good at all. I've just spoken to the hospital and they tell me the consultant is in this afternoon. He'll insist on seeing you.'

Luke shrugged. 'As long as I can be back here by tomorrow morning. I've got a very important meeting at ten-thirty.'

'Then you'll have to put it off. They'll want to keep you in overnight, at the very least.'

'I can't do that.'

201

'Nonsense, man! There's no such word as 'can't' in my book,' Sister Martin insisted.

Jenna put a restraining hand on Luke's arm. 'I know how important this meeting is to you. Perhaps I could handle it?'

'You?' Luke looked astounded.

'Why not?' Jenna gave him her sweetest, most reasonable and, if Luke did but know it, her most dangerous smile. 'After all, darling, my interest in Brackwith is every bit as great as yours, isn't it?'

'Yes, but — '

'How long will it take to brief me properly? One hour? Two? Do we have that long, Sister?'

'Sure to,' the nurse said. 'The only vehicle that can get up here at the moment is a four-wheel drive, so it'll be a question of waiting for the four-track ambulance. I'll go and sort it now.'

'Absolutely not!' thundered Luke. 'I've said I'm not — '

'Luke.' Jenna turned to him, the

warning signals in her eyes daring him to contradict her. 'You're in no position to say no. Your health must and will come first. My offer to salvage the situation is the best you'll get and, as I'm sure I don't need to remind you again, my darling,' she laid ironic emphasis on the endearment as she quite deliberately twisted her mother's wedding ring on her finger, 'that I have as great an interest in what happens to Brackwith as you do.'

'And you do trust me, don't you?' she added pointedly.

Sister Martin took Luke's silence to mean assent and bustled off to make the necessary arrangements. Conversation was impossible above the roar of the ancient Land Rover inching its way along the track at full throttle.

Jenna found herself struggling to smother a grin, in spite of the tension between them. Luke wasn't used to losing and from the grim expression on his face, he was a pretty poor loser.

When the sound of the Land Rover

had been muted by sufficient distance, he finally spoke.

'Well, can I?' he asked.

'Can you what?'

'Trust you with my plans for the John Manning Centre?'

Jenna's heart lurched as she realised the power she had over him was what she'd been hoping for, ever since she'd first arrived at Brackwith. And yet, she felt no sense of triumph.

'That depends on what they are,' she said. 'After all, you did spring them on me and I didn't get chance to look at them properly yesterday. But first things first, Luke. You look bushed. Why not rest for a while and then we'll — '

'I'll have all the rest I can handle later on,' he snarled, and Jenna had a glimpse of yet another Luke Grantley. This one was a small boy, alone and afraid, doing his best to hide his fear beneath a cloak of anger. Her heart contracted with pity for him. She was about to reach out to him but stopped. Pity was the last thing he'd want. The best way she could help him — and she was surprised at how badly she wanted to help him — would be to convince him that she could handle the site meeting.

'If you're sure. Okay, then,' she said, in her best, no-nonsense voice. 'Let's get started.'

This time she was the one who led the way along the narrow passageway to her father's study. After a pause, he followed her, and once they were perched side by side on the settle, he again handed her the folder with her father's name emblazoned on the cover. As she took it, he grasped her outstretched hand.

'Your mother's?' he asked, fingering the gold band that swivelled loosely on her finger.

Jenna felt her cheeks grow scarlet. She tried to draw her hand away so that she could take the ring off. But he held her firmly and wouldn't let her pull away.

'I never did thank you for backing me

up back there,' he said softly. 'I behaved badly again, didn't I? I told you I was an arrogant bastard, didn't I? Or was it you who told me?'

Jenna swallowed as a lump formed in her throat. 'I believe I did say something to that effect,' she said, trying but failing to summon a smile.

Luke's face, like hers, was not smiling. His eyes darkened as he lifted her hand to his lips. Then, very slowly, very gently he kissed first the finger that wore the ring and then, with infinite, agonising sweetness, kissed each of the other fingers in turn, sending a series of tingles, like tiny electric shocks, shimmering up her arm.

She bit her lip hard to hold back a soft moan. She dared not show him how much his touch affected her, and knew perfectly well that she should pull away from him, laugh or make some flippant remark to diminish the electricity that once again sparked between them, as powerful and vibrant as it had been in the barn.

Yet she did nothing, except to let a faint sigh escape her lips as he looked up at her, his eyes searching her face, as if he was trying to commit every detail of it to memory.

'Jenna. Oh, Jenna,' he whispered, shaking his head slowly, as if he was being dragged from a deep sleep. 'What kind of witch are you? What spell have you cast with those wicked emerald eyes a man could lose himself in?'

She opened her mouth but no sound came out. He placed a gentle finger under her chin and tilted her face, slowly, gently towards his. This time, she could no longer hold back as the longing for his touch swept away the last of her self-restraint. She moved towards him, relaxing into his embrace, feeling her bones turn to jelly as his strong arms closed around her.

This time, their kiss had none of the urgent, breathless passion of the kiss in the barn. Instead, it was the giving and receiving of comfort, more eloquent than any words could have been. It was shelter after a storm; sunshine after rain; comfort after pain. It was, quite simply, the most overwhelming feeling of warmth, of being cherished, that she'd ever experienced. At last, she knew, she had finally found where she belonged — and she wanted that sweet, achingly tender kiss to last forever.

Only, of course, it didn't. Eventually, agonisingly, Luke pulled back and held her at arms' length, the emotion on his face a mirror of her own.

'I love you, Luke.'

Had she really said that? Had she spoken those words aloud? Or was it that the words were filling her head, her whole body until she felt she would explode with the joy of her new, amazing discovery? She was in love with him. She was in love, really, truly, deeply in love for the first and — she knew this with utmost certainty — the last time in her life.

It was a wonderful, heady, champagne feeling.

But champagne bubbles are fragile,

insubstantial things that rise swiftly to the surface then burst. So it was with Jenna. She didn't believe in magic, or witchcraft — or love striking, unbidden, like a bolt of lightning. This couldn't be happening. More to the point, it shouldn't be happening. It was all too much, too soon. Luke had accused her of casting some sort of spell on him but, as far as she was concerned, it was the other way round.

As for telling him she loved him — it was obvious from the unchanged expression on his face that she hadn't, thank goodness, spoken the words out loud. Words formed in the heat of the moment — and what a moment! But words she couldn't possibly have meant. Could she?

She cleared her throat, but her voice still sounded strained as she said, 'I — I think we'd better concentrate on these.' She tapped the folder on the desk. 'After all, we don't have much time, do we?'

Luke stared at her for a second. Then

he manoeuvred himself awkwardly into the chair in front of the desk and opened the folder. 'Right. As you say. We don't have much time.'

How could he do that? Jenna watched him calmly spread the papers out in front of them. He was behaving as if nothing had happened between them, while she was still struggling to control the trembling in her legs and the feeling that clouds of butterflies were looping the loop inside her stomach. She was still trying to collect herself, while he was already engrossed in architects' drawings and cash flow projections. How could he behave as if nothing had happened between them?

Because nothing had. The answer hit her in the face like a wet sponge. The reason he acted as if nothing had happened was that, as far as he was concerned, it hadn't registered on his scale of momentous events. He was an attractive, well-known man, probably used to woman of all ages falling for him; probably even a little bored by it all. Her only comfort in that moment of truth, which shattered her self-esteem and made her feel like a gauche teenager, was that at least she hadn't told him aloud that she loved him.

'I thought for the next phase, we'd go for something along these lines. They're sure to ask about it, so I've put down some rough costs. See what you think.' Luke pushed a sheet filled with columns of figures towards her. Her eyes skimmed them, barely registering what she was reading.

'Wait a minute.' To her surprise, she realised her brain was capable of functioning on two quite separate levels. While one part was numbed with embarrassment, another had been reading Luke's figures, sifting and analysing them. Her professional self, the accountant that he'd found so hilarious, became intensely interested in what she was reading.

'I see what you're trying to do here,' she said, her mind now fully engaged as she became caught up by the task in hand. 'But if you showed these projections in another way, they'd be far more impressive, not to say meaningful. Did you compile these yourself? If so, can you show me the spreadsheet?'

Luke turned on the laptop and Jenna waited as he called up the spreadsheet. She dragged the settle closer as he pushed the laptop towards her. Her fingers flew over the keys as she focussed on the columns of figures that rippled across the screen as if they were dancing to her tune.

'And then,' she said when the columns had finally settled, 'You could do this.' She pressed another couple of keys. 'And then this. What do you think?' With a flourish, she took the paper from the printer and handed it to him. 'Well? Do you think the men in suits will go for it?'

He read the paper in careful silence, pausing several times to go back over something, nodding approval as he did so. When he finished, he looked at her with a dawning respect.

'I'm impressed — very impressed. May I?' He placed the paper in the folder. 'And could you show what would happen if we budgeted for this? Or maybe . . . ?'

★   ★   ★

For the next couple of hours, they worked together and Jenna enjoyed the subtle change in Luke's attitude towards her. Before, he'd been showing her what the project was about, telling her of his plans. But now, they worked together as equals, engaged on a project that engrossed them both.

'Well?' she asked, unable to resist it any longer. 'Will I do, do you think? Do you still think my accountancy training is a joke? Or have I managed to convince you of my competence?'

'Fishing for compliments again?' he said, laughing gently. 'Poor Jenna. I shouldn't tease you but it's so rare

213

these days to come across someone who blushes as readily as you do, I just can't resist it.'

'I'm glad I'm an object of such amusement to you,' she retorted stiffly, feeling every inch the awkward teenager again.

'You're many things to me, Jenna Manning, but not one of them is an object of amusement,' he said, so quietly that she had to strain to hear as his face grew serious. 'One day, perhaps, I'll tell you what they all are.'

'What's wrong with now?' Her voice, too, was hardly more than a whisper as she saw something in his eyes that allowed her a flicker of hope. 'Go on,' she urged. 'Tell me now.'

Luke looked down at her, his expression unreadable. Then he turned away, too quickly, catching his breath against the wave of pain that crashed over him as he reached for his crutches.

'I'm sorry. It's . . . This is wrong. I'm so sorry. If I thought — '

He stopped as they both became

aware of the sound of a big, powerful vehicle slowly making its way along the track towards the house.

The ambulance had arrived.

13

'Luke.' She placed a gentle hand on his arm and felt him stiffen as she did so. 'It'll be all right. Everything will be fine, you'll see.'

'Oh, I see.' He scowled. 'So you were an orthopaedic surgeon before becoming a trainee accountant, were you?'

Jenna pulled her hand away as if stung. 'I'm sorry,' she said. 'I didn't mean — '

'Oh no,' he groaned. 'Jenna, I'm the one who's sorry. God knows, you're only trying to help — '

'It's okay. You don't have to apologise. I understand,' she said, quietly — as, indeed, she did. After nursing her mother all those long months, she knew how pain and fear could eat away at a person, making them ready to hit out at anyone or anything.

'I'll come in to the hospital and see

you tomorrow, shall I?' she offered. 'After the meeting, of course, then I can let you know how it went.'

'Fine,' he said, but Jenna felt he'd closed her out and was not really listening to her.

Only when the ambulance pulled to a stop did he look at her with something more like his normal expression.

'I do appreciate what you're doing, you know.' He smiled, the harsh lines that had set on his face softening as he did so. 'Are you sure you'll be all right here on your own? It's a big ask — and I can't help thinking that you'd be better off going to stay in a hotel somewhere.'

'Don't worry on my account. This place was my home when you were in short trousers.' If she was honest, she was quite looking forward to having Brackwith to herself for a bit, hoping it would give her some much-needed thinking time. 'I'll be quite safe here and the only ghosts here are good ones,' she rattled on. 'Besides — who will look after your cat if I'm not here?'

'My cat — his name's Tommy, by the way — is not my cat at all, but belongs in one of those cottages at the head of the valley. As soon as he's on his own, he returns to his own home, I promise you. I've been in touch with the owners on several occasions. They have three other cats which, they reckon, is why he goes AWOL every now and again. They're quite relaxed about the arrangement as long as I am, they say. And he's good company, actually.'

Jenna thought of Tommy's comforting presence at the foot of her bed for the last few nights and smiled. 'He is indeed.'

'I hope you won't be too bored. If you are, there's a folder on my desk with some notes I made for your father's biography. See what you think. You may be able to add some of your own, to give another perspective which could be useful.'

'I thought you didn't want me to

touch anything on your desk. Remember?' She couldn't resist teasing him.

'That was when I thought you were some nosy-parker journalist,' he said wryly. 'But — '

'And how do you know I'm not?' She laughed. 'How do you know I wasn't a journalist — between being a surgeon and accountant, of course?'

His laughing response was interrupted by the arrival of the paramedics and their laughter died abruptly.

'Oh Jenna,' he whispered as he reached for her hand and pulled it to his lips. 'I wish . . . I wish I'd met you before . . . '

★   ★   ★

For a long time after the ambulance had driven away, Jenna sat at the table, staring down at her hands. She could still feel the cool, feather-light touch of his lips, the pressure of his fingers where he'd squeezed hers in a silent goodbye. She looked, too, at her mother's wedding ring and remembered how he'd trailed a line of kisses across her fingers. She checked her watch for the twentieth time in as many minutes and wondered how far they were now, and whether the jolting journey along the stony track had hurt him.

She left the kitchen to the sleeping cat and went in to her father's — no, she corrected herself — Luke's study. It still felt strange to be in the familiar yet subtly different room. Again, she felt her father's presence very strongly, but this time she felt Luke's as well.

She prowled about, picking out some of her father's books. Then she crossed to the bookcase containing the books written by Luke.

She picked out one and let her gaze linger over the author's photograph on the back of the dust jacket. It showed Luke in climbing gear but without a helmet, head thrown back, eyes screwed up against the sun, looking up at a distant summit. It was a powerful picture and Jenna could see the excitement on his face as he savoured the challenge ahead.

She took the book to the deep-cushioned chair she remembered with such affection from her childhood. She burrowed among the saggy cushions, tucking her legs beneath her, opened the book and began to read.

She meant to make herself some coffee, but forgot. She meant, too, to make herself some lunch, but lunch-time too went by unnoticed. So, too, did the time for afternoon tea. In fact, she was so engrossed in the book she lost all sense of time and it was not until Tommy stalked in, tail rigid, green eyes fixed intently on her, that she realised it had grown dark and was way past the cat's — and her — feeding time.

Reluctantly, she put the book down, rubbed her stiff legs and followed the indignant cat into the kitchen. She did a double time-check. Nearly six o'clock. She couldn't believe she'd spent the best part of a day curled up with a book.

Yet what a book! It was a thriller, set against a mountaineering background, exciting and well-paced, driving as relentlessly as an avalanche towards the nail-biting climax. Luke was indeed a talented writer, showing a sensitivity and depth of feeling for his characters and their problems. He was also a man in love — in love with the mountains, just as her father had been. And that love lit up his writing.

As she spooned cat food into the bowl, she realised with a guilty start that she'd been so engrossed in the book, she hadn't looked at Luke's notes. She placed the cat's dish on the floor, then hurried back to the study. This time, she resisted the temptation of the open book and went instead to the desk.

She hesitated before opening the folder. She still had so many conflicting emotions about her father that, for a moment, she was tempted to return to the novel for another dose of blessed escapism.

Instead she reached for the first page of notes. *Luke made a point of telling me about them,* she told herself. *The least I can do is read them.*

She found reading the notes confusing and painful. Luke was writing of the time soon after the divorce, and it seemed to Jenna as if the man she was reading about and the man she knew as her father was not the same person. Who was the real John Manning? The exciting but shadowy figure she remembered from before the divorce? The selfish man who was always breaking promises that he became after? Or the strong, dependable friend of Luke's memory? Which of these three was the real John Manning? She'd expected some discrepancies between her recollections and Luke's. They were, after all, looking at him from different viewpoints. But such huge differences? What could account for that?

Not what, of course, but who. Some

words of Luke's forced her at last to see things with devastating clarity.

'Your mother was wrong about many things,' she remembered him saying. 'She was wrong about your father. She was even wrong about me — but, most of all, I'm beginning to suspect, she was wrong about you.'

Why hadn't she thought this through before? Why had she always pushed her suspicions about her mother to the back of her mind? Why had she been so quick to make excuses for her?

Because she was a coward, that was why.

But there was another, more painful reason. If she was forced to admit that the unreliable, promise-breaking father of her memory was in fact not true but a result of her mother's manipulation, then where did that leave her? Yes, her mother had behaved appallingly — but so, too, had she. She, Jenna, had treated her father very badly indeed. She'd rejected him, ignored his letters, 'forgotten' to return his calls. In short, she'd quite deliberately cut him out of her life after the night of the concert and if, in the process she'd hurt him, well, she could justify that to herself on the grounds of how badly he'd hurt her.

But what if he hadn't *knowingly* hurt her? The discovery that he had not broken his promises and that he'd had every intention of coming to the concert that night, but that her mother had prevented him from doing so by deliberately telling him a lie, was almost too much to bear.

How could her mother do such a cruel and terrible thing to them both? Why? How could she let a small child of ten, eleven, twelve years believe that the father whom she'd adored had simply stopped loving her? Was that all she'd been to her mother — one more weapon with which to hurt John Manning, the man who, when asked to choose between his wife and his climbing career, had chosen the mountains?

She searched among the papers on

top of Luke's desk and found the one written by her mother that she'd come across before. She hesitated before opening it, even though she had a pretty good idea by now what was going to be in it.

Luke was, of course, quite right. The letter was short, sharp and to the point and written a couple of months ago. It said, quite simply, that Lynda would maybe consider selling her share in Brackwith if Luke would increase his offer.

Why did she do that? How did she think she was going to get away with selling a property that wasn't hers to sell? And when, if ever, was she going to tell Jenna?

Then Jenna realised what her mother had been up to. She probably had no intention of selling the property — how could she? It was much more likely that she was merely playing with Luke, putting delays in his way, trying to cause him as much inconvenience as possible.

Jenna looked up. It was dark outside and her reflection showed up ghostlike in the window. Once again, she heard Luke's voice inside her head.

'She was wrong about your father . . . She was even wrong about me.'

Jenna gasped. 'If she misled me about Dad, surely she was also wrong about Luke?'

Her heart gave a convulsive leap of joy. If that was the case, then surely Luke wasn't to blame for her father's death?

The joy of that discovery lifted her mood like a shaft of sunlight piercing a cloud. She went back to reading Luke's notes with a lighter heart and now found that, instead of being wracked with guilt and regret, she was enjoying the process of getting to know her father through Luke's eyes and words.

Once again, she had to admit that she'd been wrong about Luke. This time, it was over her assertion that he'd been too close to her father to be able to write about him objectively. For within those pages of rough notes, she felt he'd already succeeded in capturing the essence of the complicated man who had been her father.

As she turned the next page, a slip of paper fell out and she recognised her father's handwriting. It was a letter he'd written to Luke, inviting him to go climbing in the Alps with him.

I know this is a difficult time for you to get away, the letter had said. *And under normal circumstances I wouldn't dream of asking you. But these are not normal circumstances and there's something I must do, where timing is of the utmost importance.*

A shiver of horror ran its cold finger down her back as Jenna looked at the date at the top of the page. The trip referred to was the one from which Luke had returned alone.

I hoped Jenna could have come with us, she read on. *But, once again, I'm afraid it's not to be. It's a pity because I was hoping the two of you could meet at last. I would have liked that very much indeed.*

Jenna bit down hard on her clenched knuckles. What had Luke said? ' . . . I wish we'd met sooner . . . '

'*You* wish, Luke?' she whispered to the empty room, as she remembered how many invitations from her father she'd turned down in the last couple of years of his life. Her hurt and anger towards him after his no-show at the concert, drip-fed by her mother. In particular, she remembered the last invitation. The one to go climbing with him, and how there was someone he'd dearly like her to meet. She'd automatically assumed that he wanted her to meet a woman, maybe even introduce her as her future stepmother — and, although she had, rationally, accepted the fact that her parents' marriage was over, there was still a little part of her that had dared to hope.

Now, she realised, the someone he wanted her to meet must have been Luke. If only.

You can't wish that as much as I do, Luke, she went on, as her thoughts led to their inevitable, bitter conclusion. *If we'd met then, maybe we'd have hit it off, who knows? But maybe too, if I'd come on that last expedition, as he'd wanted me to, he would still be alive.*

If she'd gone with her father and Luke that summer, they wouldn't have attempted the difficult Alpine route — not with such an inexperienced climber as herself in the party.

She was, she realised, as much to blame as anyone for her father's death.

If only I'd gone.

If only. Those two small words were surely the saddest, the most futile in the English language.

★ ★ ★

'He's asleep,' the young nurse said. 'But I'm sure it's all right for you to go on in.'

Jenna let herself in to the small side room, closing the door quietly behind her as she did so, anxious not to disturb Luke. As she watched the even rise and fall of his breathing, she wanted to go and find someone, to ask what had happened, but now she was here she couldn't bear to leave him.

Eventually, his eyes opened and he frowned as if trying to work out where he was or who she was.

'Luke?' her voice was tentative. 'How are you feeling?'

'Bloody awful,' he said, then his eyes began to clear. 'Did you get here safely? Are the roads all right?'

'They're fine,' she reassured him. 'They've been well gritted. But the important thing is, how are you? Have they told you anything yet?'

A shadow chased across his face. 'I'll live,' he said grimly, then changed the subject. 'Tell me about the site meeting. How did it go?'

'Everything seemed to go very well indeed. I took them up and showed them the Upper Barn and the other outbuildings, then brought them back to the house and showed them the plans and the figures. They seemed impressed and, I'm glad to say, asked all the right questions as if they were genuinely interested in what we — I mean, in what you are trying to do.'

'Did they say when we'll hear from them?'

'Within the month. The next planning meeting is February the twelfth and we should hear soon after that.'

She looked down at her hands. She was aware that Luke was watching her closely but making no attempt to break the silence that had fallen.

Jenna had so much she wanted to say. She'd gone over and over it all last night and then again during the drive to the hospital. But first, she had to know about his operation, although she had a feeling it was not good news.

'Have they told you anything?' she asked.

'Nothing I hadn't already worked out for myself,' he said dismissively. 'So, tell me, what have you been doing with yourself? Are you remembering to feed the cat? One missed meal and he goes back home, you know.'

'I'm afraid I nearly caused him to pack his bags yesterday because I was so engrossed in your book I forgot the time. I really enjoyed it.'

'Which one was it?'

'*Above The Snow Line.*'

'That was my first. I have your father to thank for that. He was the one who encouraged me to keep at it, even when I convinced myself that I didn't have what it takes to write a novel. Did you notice that I dedicated the book to him?'

'I did. And, Luke, I also read your notes.'

'Good. Did you add any of your own?'

Jenna hesitated. She couldn't sit here

and make conversation with him any longer as if nothing had happened. Either she'd have to say what she'd rehearsed, or leave. She hadn't spent all this time trying to work out what to say to him to chicken out now.

She took a deep breath and went for it. 'Reading your notes made me do some hard thinking — about my father, my mother but, most of all, about myself.'

14

'And the result of all this thinking?' Luke asked evenly, his eyes giving nothing away.

'I think — no, I know — that my mother was wrong. And — and that I was wrong, too.'

'Wrong about what?'

'I was wrong about my father, what I thought of him, the way I treated him. But most of all, Luke, I was wrong about you.'

Luke's steady gaze held hers. 'Well, I know how you were wrong about your father. But in what way do you think you were wrong about me?'

Jenna flinched, but forced herself not to look away. 'I've been thinking a lot about my mother and the way she — ' She stopped and looked down at her mother's wedding ring, now returned to her right hand. 'Do you know, I've only just realised this, but it's quite extraordinary when you think about it. Mum continued to wear her wedding ring even after the divorce. She professed to hate Dad, certainly acted as if she did, yet she wore his ring until the day she died. As if, deep down, in spite of everything, she still loved him. Don't you think that's extraordinary?'

'There's a thin line between love and hate,' he said. 'Besides, your mother struck me as a lady who hated to let go of anything.'

'I wonder if that was it,' Jenna said, almost to herself. 'I've tried, you see, to work out why she did what she did, why she poisoned my mind — and James's too, of course — against Dad and, later on, against you. I think I've worked it out about Dad. She'd been on at him for years, as long as I can remember, in fact, to give up climbing, but he always said no. Until, one day, she forced him to choose between her and the mountains — and he chose the mountains.'

'It wasn't quite that clear-cut,' Luke

said. 'That's still your mother's version.'

'Oh? Are you saying that he didn't make that choice?'

'Jenna, there was no choice. John was a climber. It was what he was, a part of him. Asking him to give it up was like asking him to give up breathing, or using his right arm.'

'But he still put climbing before his family,' she persisted. 'However you word it, that's what he did. My mother, rightly or wrongly, asked him to give it up. She used to get so uptight when he was away. Then, when Rob was killed in the Himalayas — remember Rob Williamson? — well, Dad should have been on the expedition, but couldn't go for some reason and Rob took his place. It was after that that Mum forced him to choose.'

Luke said nothing but shifted into a more comfortable position on the narrow bed.

'I wanted you to see things from her point of view for a change,' she said, nervously pleating and repleating the scarf that she'd taken from her neck and placed in her lap. 'She was bringing up two young children, most of the time on her own, whilst at the same time worried sick about her husband. She told me she was sure each climb would be his last, that it was only a matter of time before his luck ran out, which, of course, was exactly what did happen in the end, wasn't it?'

Just like yours has, she could have added, but didn't. During the past few days her belief system seemed to have been taken out, shaken and put back together again in a different order and she was now less sure of her own opinions and more prepared to think before she spoke — especially where Luke was concerned.

'Is that how you see what happened to your father? That his luck ran out?' His voice had a roughness to it that made it the voice of a stranger.

'I don't think — ' Jenna began, but thought better of it. 'Look, this isn't the time or the place to be discussing this, is it? We'll talk about it some other time.'

'But you were the one who insisted on this conversation, remember? I was happy to go on talking about the cat, Brackwith or any other cosy topic. But no, you said you'd been doing some hard thinking, that you were wrong about something. Now, that's got to be worth following up. Something tells me it's not often you admit to being in the wrong.'

Jenna's nervous fingers stilled and the scarf slipped unnoticed to the floor. Her troubled eyes scanned his face, hoping to see he was teasing her. But this time, there was no glimpse of laughter in those storm-cloud eyes. His expression was as serious as her own, but there was something else, too, something that made her want to run away, whilst at the same time ensuring she didn't.

'I was wrong about my father,' she began in a low voice, looking down at her hands now empty in her lap, her fingers twisting against each other now that they no longer had the scarf. 'I shouldn't have let my mother . . . I shouldn't have believed her. I should have thought things through for myself. If I had, then Dad and I could have sorted things out. If I had — ' She looked up, eyes brimming. 'Then maybe he'd still be alive.'

Luke's face went rigid. Whatever he'd been expecting, it obviously wasn't that. His expression was one of such total bewilderment that at any other time, she would have found it rather funny.

'How the devil do you work that out?' he asked, still in the same harsh voice.

Jenna explained about reading the letter she'd found among his notes. 'I hope you don't mind,' she said. 'I thought as you'd invited me to read your notes, it would be okay. It was, wasn't it?' she added, troubled by his grim expression. But she couldn't stop now. She had to go on, whatever his reaction.

'It was,' he said tersely. 'Go on.'

'I remember Dad asking me to go climbing with him that summer, and I can't remember what crass, stupid excuse I came up with for not going, but — '

'You were hoping to go on a riding holiday with one of your school friends.'

Jenna flushed. 'You see? A crass, stupid excuse. I was still trying to hurt him, to pay him back for hurting me. Oh, if only I hadn't. If only I'd yelled, called him an unreliable bastard, screamed at him for letting me down the night of the concert and all the other times, anything to provoke him into defending himself, to make him explain what had really happened. If only I'd done that — '

'Jenna, there's no point in this.' His voice cut through her self-recrimination. 'What you did or didn't do made no difference to the final outcome. He would still have died.'

'But don't you see? If I'd gone as he wanted me to, you'd have gone somewhere else, somewhere less dangerous, because of me. You wouldn't

241

have — ' She checked herself. 'He'd still be alive.'

'So tell me.' His voice was still harsh, but now very quiet, very controlled. 'What do you know about your father's death? How do you think he died?'

A silence so heavy it was almost tangible fell across the room. It was as if all the usual bustle and noise of the busy hospital was frozen in that single moment.

This was it. This was what she'd come to tell him. Whatever happened after this, whether or not his operation was successful, or whatever ever happened to his plans for Brackwith, there would be no hope of any sort of future for them — if indeed there was — until this had been sorted out. She'd lost her father because she'd failed to speak out. She wasn't going to make the same mistake again.

It had all seemed so easy, rehearsing in front of the bathroom mirror at Brackwith.

'You must realise, Luke,' she began in

a subdued voice, 'I grew up in the shadow of mountains, my mother's fear of them, my father's love for them. When Dad died the bitterness Mum felt towards the mountains — his obsession, she called it — became mixed up and transferred to — ' She swallowed and paused in an attempt to pull her thoughts together. This was much more difficult than she'd imagined and Luke wasn't making things any easier for her, sitting there like a . . . like a lump of granite.

'I'm sorry. I'm not putting this very well,' she said. 'I'm trying to explain what I meant when I said I'd been wrong about you. When — when Dad died I was ill for several weeks, flu, or something, and don't remember much about it, only what Mum told me. And she said that, on Dad's last climb, he'd had a fall and that you . . . that you . . . '

'Go on.'

She drew in a lungful of air. 'Mum told me that you left him there, that you

243

could have saved him but didn't. That when eventually you got help, you gave the rescue team the wrong bearings so that by the time they reached him, it was too late.'

She looked up at his face and what she saw there made her reach for his hand.

'Oh, Luke, I'm so sorry,' she cried. 'I can't say I didn't believe her because that wouldn't be true. I had no reason not to. But as soon as I — ' she stopped. For one crazy moment, she'd been on the verge of saying 'as soon as I fell in love with you' and quickly changed it to 'As soon as I got to know you, I knew she was wrong, that it was another of her sick lies. It couldn't have happened the way she said, could it? You loved him, too. So why, Luke? Why did she do it? Why did she hate you so much?'

He said nothing. Through his long silence Jenna gradually became aware of the outside world again, of the noise and bustle from the adjoining wards rising above the sound of her own anxious heartbeat. Dishes clattered, a vacuum cleaner droned and, in the distance, an ambulance siren wailed while a child squealed with delight. Jenna held her breath as she waited for him to speak, but finally could bear it no longer.

'Luke, for pity's sake!' Her voice was sharp. 'Answer me. Why did my mother say those awful things about you?'

'Because they're true.'

For the first stunned second she was sure she'd misheard. 'What?'

'I said they're true.' His eyes were a chilling ice blue as they turned towards her. 'Your mother hated me because she believed I was responsible for your father's death. And although she was wrong about many things, in that particular instance she was right. Everything she told you about what happened that day was true.'

'But you don't know the awful things she said. She told me you went off and left him to die. That can't be true.' She shook her head. 'I know you wouldn't do that. This is a game, some kind of silly test.'

'It's no game, Jenna. Oh sure, the enquiry exonerated me, but they were wrong,' he said. 'They were wrong and your mother was right. I, and nobody else, am responsible for your father's death. I should have stayed with him, waited with him until help arrived. But I didn't. I thought I could get help to him quicker by going down on my own.'

'But . . . ' Jenna was stunned. She didn't want to believe him and yet the expression on his face told her more eloquently than any words that he was speaking the truth. He had the look of a man haunted by what he'd done — or rather, by what he had not done. She felt no pity for him, though, not any more, as all the old hatred and resentment resurfaced.

'How did someone as experienced as you give the rescue team the wrong bearings?'

'I've asked myself that question a million times and the answer is, I don't know. When we got back, John wasn't where I thought I'd left him. I assumed I'd made a mistake.'

'A mistake?' Jenna stood up and turned quickly away from him. As she did so, she felt the room swim in front of her and made a grab for the back of the chair. She forced herself to breathe deeply. The last thing she wanted was to fall in a dead faint at his feet.

'Why?' She rounded on him, her throat tight with barely suppressed fury. 'Why did you leave him there? Was she right after all? Was it to save your own miserable skin? How could you, Luke? How could you? He was worth a million of you.'

'Indeed he was.' His quiet voice was a marked contrast to hers. 'And don't you think I don't ask myself that same question every day of my life? He was, as you say, worth a million of me.'

Jenna wished she could have unsaid those last angry words. It was kicking a man when he was down. And yet — and yet ... She paused, looked down at him, and hardened her heart. If he thought she was going to apologise, he was going to be disappointed.

'I'll leave it to our respective solicitors to deal with the sale of my share of Brackwith,' she said coldly. 'There should be no need for any further contact between us.'

'Where are you going?'

'That's none of your damn business, is it?'

She walked to the door but he called her back. She turned, for some wild, stupid moment thinking, hoping he was going to tell her it had all been a terrible mistake.

'I think there's something you should know,' he said. 'Who knows, it might even make you feel better.'

Jenna knew with absolute certainty there was nothing he could say that would make her feel better. Nevertheless, she turned back in to the room, her heart thudding.

'Yes?'

'When you first came in, you asked me what the consultant said, remember? And I told you it was nothing that I didn't already know.'

Jenna remembered. It seemed a lifetime ago.

'In view of what has happened,' he went on, 'No doubt you'll be pleased to hear that the early results are not looking good. There are some more tests to be done later but he's not hopeful. I'll probably never regain full mobility in my legs and there's a good chance I'll end up in a wheelchair for good within five years.'

Jenna felt as if the breath had been punched out of her. So many awful things, she couldn't cope with them. She had to get away. But she couldn't move. His voice, so calm, so quiet, so terrible, held her. And he hadn't finished with her yet.

'Your mother once told me I'd pay for what I'd done,' he said. 'That one day she'd have her revenge. Well, today, it seems, is pay day.' He smiled, but it was a bitter travesty of a smile — the memory of which would stay with her for the rest of her life.

'Remember this. Your father died on a crisp, clear mountain doing what he loved most in the whole world. I have to die little by little, trapped inside a useless body, one that soon won't even get me up a flight of stairs, least of all a mountain. How's that for sweet revenge? What a pity your mother didn't live long enough to see it.'

Jenna stumbled from the room. In her haste to get away, she almost cannoned into a slender, dark-haired woman, who was standing by the nurses' station. Jenna muttered an apology but the other woman, her face creased with anxiety, was too focussed on trying to catch the attention of a nurse, who was busily tapping away at a keyboard, to respond.

'I'm Julia Grantley,' she was saying. 'I called earlier and was told that the doctor would want to talk to me before

I went in to see Luke.'

Jenna had thought Luke couldn't possibly hurt her any more than he'd already done that day. But the knowledge that he'd lied to her, that he'd denied the fact that he was married, hurt beyond belief.

15

'Sarah? Have you seen this?' Jenna stared in amazement at the sight that greeted her as she walked in to the small, dark kitchen. The cherry tree in the back garden was a riot of pink marshmallow blossom. 'When did this happen?'

Sarah shuffled into the kitchen, still rubbing sleep from her eyes. She blinked at the tree. 'That's what happens to people like you who work too many long hours,' she said with a grin. 'Spring arrives and they miss it.'

Spring? Already? Jenna used to love spring, with its promise of new beginnings, but not any more. Now she found the only way to cope with life was to live in the present. The past was firmly closed and the future as grey as a wet Monday morning.

She'd been in London a little over

two months now, driving straight down from Cumbria that terrible day at the hospital. Her heart still lurched at the memory. If Julia hadn't turned up at that moment, Jenna wouldn't have made it as far as the hospital car park before turning back and telling Luke that her father's death was a terrible accident and that she no longer blamed him. That it didn't matter what happened to his legs; not to her, at least. That she'd always be there for him.

Then she saw his wife, Julia, and ran out to the car park, jumping into her car and stopping only briefly at Brackwith to pick up her things and call Steven. Then she'd driven straight down to London.

'If you need a friend,' Steven had said and she'd taken him at his word. The job he'd phoned her about earlier was filled, but he'd found her a temporary job with one of his clients that was exactly what she needed — a demanding job with long hours that didn't leave her time to think.

Steven had, indeed, been a true friend, never once asking what went wrong in Cumbria — although sometimes he'd ask if she was going to resume her studies, and therefore, the implication went, her life. But he made no attempt to persuade her when she put the decision off yet again.

He'd also introduced her to his colleague, Sarah, who owned a tiny Victorian terraced house and was happy to let her spare room. The two women formed an immediate friendship.

Sarah handed Jenna a coffee. 'Don't you love Saturdays?' She gave a catlike stretch. 'Steven and I are going to try that new Thai restaurant for lunch. Fancy coming?'

Jenna shook her head. 'I won't, thanks. I've got piles of washing to do.'

'Jenna?' Sarah put her hand on Jenna's arm. 'You are all right about me and Steven, aren't you? I mean, I know that you and he were . . . '

'All right? I'm delighted. Steven's been a great friend, the best, and I don't know what I'd have done without him. But that's all he is — a very good, very dear friend. I couldn't be more pleased about you and him.'

'Good. In that case, prove it by coming to lunch with us. You know how you enjoy Thai food, and the place has had some great reviews.'

Jenna allowed herself to be persuaded. The restaurant was almost full when they arrived and they threaded their way with difficulty among the tightly-packed tables. Ahead of them was a couple so engrossed in each other that Jenna felt a pang of envy. The woman looked up, as if aware of her gaze.

Jenna stopped abruptly.

It was Julia Grantley. And the man holding her hand and gazing deep into her eyes was not Luke.

Jenna backed away, thankful that they hadn't seen her. She muttered a quick apology to Sarah and Steven and hurried out, striding blindly along the crowded pavements until, eventually, the shock and anger began to subside. On the other side of the road was a park, not the manicured type where neat flowers grew to regulation height, but a place where hawthorn bushes sprawled and fat-budded horse chestnut trees huddled like children sharing a secret. Where the turf felt soft and springy after the hardness of the pavements.

The sight of Julia had shattered Jenna's fragile peace, making her ask questions she'd vowed she'd never ask again. Questions like, was Luke's marriage over? If so, how did she feel about it?

And the big one: how did she feel about Luke?

She walked on, thoughts and emotions twisting and spinning around in her mind like tights in a washing machine until, suddenly, she noticed a man on a bench in front of her. He was leaning forward, his shoulders hunched, his straight black hair ruffled by the gentle spring breeze.

At first, she thought it was a trick of her mind. She'd been thinking so hard about Luke that a stranger in the distance had seemed to look exactly like him. She was less than three feet away before she could see without a doubt that it was indeed him — but by then, she was so shocked by his appearance that her instinct to run away had vanished.

He'd lost weight and his face, once lean, now looked gaunt. The bruises had gone but the still-angry scar emphasised his too-prominent cheek-bones. But it was his eyes that shocked her most. She'd seen them darken with pain, blaze with anger and soften with — she pushed that particular memory aside. Whatever the emotion, they'd always been full of life.

Now they were dull and told of pain-filled days and nights. They were the eyes of a man who'd been to hell and back.

'Luke?' She approached him hesitantly. 'What are you doing here, in London?'

For a second, his surprise at seeing her rekindled the light in his eyes, but it faded as swiftly as it had flared.

'I might ask you the same question,' he said as he reached for his crutches. He would have stood up had Jenna not hastily sat down beside him. In truth she would have preferred a greater distance between them, but she didn't want to oblige him to struggle to his feet.

'I asked first.' She smiled, but he did not smile back.

'I'm going into hospital tomorrow, here in London. Julia thinks it's worth another go.'

At the sound of Julia's name, Jenna stiffened. 'Well,' she answered in an over-bright voice, 'you've got to give it a go. After all, you never know, do you?'

'Oh, I think I do,' he said, in the dead voice of someone who has given up hope. 'I rather think I do.'

'Luke . . . in the hospital . . . what I said . . . ' Jenna blurted out. Something about him terrified her and made her want to put things right between them. She drew breath, ignored his lack of response and lurched on. 'Those awful things I said to you . . . I should never have said them. They were words that would have been better left unsaid.'

'But you thought them.' He turned to watch a blackbird as it flew, scolding, from the bushes to the side of them. 'And, unless I'm much mistaken, you still do. Isn't that so?'

The direct question caught her unawares.

'Well, no, of course not. I don't — '

'Of course you do. Why else would you have sent back the extra five thousand pounds I paid you for your share in Brackwith, with nothing more than a short note from your solicitor?'

Jenna flushed and looked down at her hands. 'It wasn't the amount we'd agreed.' Poor Mr Bennington; she'd had to force him to write that note. 'I told you at the time I wouldn't accept the extra. But I'm sorry if my refusal offended you.'

Their eyes held. Luke was first to look away, his gaze returning to the blackbird.

'You didn't answer my question,' he said. 'What are you doing here?'

'I live here,' she said, adding quickly when she saw one black eyebrow raise with surprise, 'Well, not here exactly. Down in the less affluent part. A trainee accountant's salary doesn't run to the properties around here,' she added with a rueful grin.

He turned and grabbed her forearm. 'He's not right for you, Jenna!' he said in a harsh voice, 'For Heaven's sake, woman, surely you can see that for yourself.'

'What on earth are you talking about?'

'This accountant, Steven, that's his name, isn't it? He's not right for you. You're making a mistake, surely you can see that?'

'Not right for me?' Indignantly she pushed his hand from her arm. 'And who *is* right for me? You? An affair with a married man? Is that right for me?'

'Your father was a good friend to me and if I can be half as good a friend to you — ' Luke's eyes had come alive and were now the ice storm she remembered so well. 'No, don't walk away, Jenna, not this time. Hear me out,' he said as she stood up. 'Look, I've a flat near here. Why don't we go there and talk, about you and me and where we go from here? And I need to tell you about Julia — '

Jenna was appalled at how close she'd come to giving herself away. For a crazy moment, her heart had leapt with joy that he thought there was something between them worth discussing. She'd even told herself that if friendship was all he was offering, then she'd take it. Anything was better than the past two months of awful nothingness. But that was before he mentioned Julia.

'How dare you use me!' she hissed,

her green eyes ablaze with anger. 'You pretend to offer me friendship when all you really want is to get even with your unfaithful wife, who as we speak is draped all over her latest boyfriend in the restaurant I've just left. Well, I can do without friends like you, thank you. Steven's a better friend than you'll ever be.'

She started to walk away — then turned back, appalled at what she'd done and worried by his unnatural stillness.

'I shouldn't have blurted it out like that. Forgive me.'

Luke said nothing.

'Look, I'd better go, Luke. Nothing I can say will make you feel any better and the chances are, I'll only say something that will make you feel worse. Will you be all right?'

'I'll be fine.'

'Would you like me to fetch — to tell Julia — ?'

'No,' he snapped. 'I don't need Julia. I don't need anyone. I'm fine.'

'So, it's Luke versus The World again, is it?' she said softly, then shook her head as he looked at her, puzzled. 'It doesn't matter, I'll go. And Luke, I am sorry for telling you like that. It was a cruel, wicked thing to do. I hope things go well for you tomorrow. Goodbye.'

She walked quickly away, eyes filled with tears. She thought she heard him call after her but kept walking, never looking back until she reached Sarah's house.

★　★　★

As she let herself in, the phone was ringing but she let the answering machine pick it up.

It was her brother, James. 'Oh for Heaven's sake,' she heard him grumble. 'I hate these wretched things. Jen, if you're there, pick up the damn phone. It's terribly important. I — '

'I'm here, James. What's the problem?'

'Oh, thank goodness. The thing is,

I've just heard from old Bennington that the people buying the cottage want completion next week. And we haven't been down to clear the place out — '

'I've been ready to do it for weeks, as well you know. You're the one who's been putting it off.'

'Yes, I know, but — '

'Well, now we can't put it off any longer. I'll pick you up first thing tomorrow and we'll — '

'That's what I've been trying to tell you. I'm leaving for Germany tomorrow. Last-minute thing, I'm afraid. I'll be gone for at least two weeks. I'm really sorry.'

As it happened, a few days scrubbing floors and turning out cupboards back in Somerset, safely out of the way of Luke and Julia and, more immediately, Steven and Sarah and their questions, was exactly what Jenna needed. So, although she grumbled at James and his habit of running away when faced with anything unpleasant, she packed her things, left a note for Sarah and a

264

phone message for her boss, and set off on the drive from London to Somerset with a sense of relief.

★ ★ ★

It was late afternoon when she arrived. The cottage had an abandoned air. James had already taken all his personal possessions, and Jenna spent the evening sorting out her own things, putting off dealing with her mother's belongings for as long as she could.

It was Sunday evening, almost twenty-four hours after her arrival, before she forced herself to do so.

The sound of the church bells ringing for Evensong drifted up from the village as she hesitated at the door to her mother's bedroom. Would she feel her presence in the way that she'd felt her father's?

As she entered the room, she knew at once that her mother wasn't there. It was filled only with the pathetic remnants of her small life. Jenna sat at the elegant walnut dressing table, still stacked with the bottles of perfume and body lotions that Lynda had loved so much, and felt only pity for the unhappy woman her mother had been.

She placed the bottles, one by one, in a black plastic sack. Then she crossed to the small antique desk beneath the window, unfolded yet another sack and began to clear the drawers. Old electricity bills, birthday cards, shopping lists. Her mother had squirrelled them all away.

The third drawer was a surprise, however. Instead of a mass of papers like the first two, it was empty except for a broken pen, two rubber bands — and an envelope with 'Jenna' written on it in her mother's hand.

Jenna thought of the other posthumous letter she'd received from her mother. It would have been much better, she thought bitterly, had she never seen that — never known about Brackwith, or met Luke Grantley.

She stared at the envelope for a long

time. She wanted to drop it, unopened, into the sack along with the birthday cards and phone bills. But she couldn't.

Better to get it over with, then. She took a deep breath and tore open the envelope — which contained another envelope.

As she opened it, her hands were shaking so much that she could hardly make out her father's bold, sloping handwriting.

16

My dearest Jenna, he'd written. *This is the most difficult thing I've ever written and I'll leave it to your mother to decide when she gives this to you, although I hope it will be sooner rather than later.*

'Oh, Dad,' she whispered. 'If you only knew how much, much later.'

This is not my usual sort of expedition, the letter went on, *for the simple reason that it's my last. I will not be coming back. You see, my dear, I have cancer and it's gone too far for treatment. I don't want to die in a hospital bed, Jenna. I've always said I wanted to die up here, in the mountains, doing what I love. So I'm going to walk out in the snow, to where I know Luke and the rescue party won't find me until it's too late. It will be an easy way out for me, but a coward's way. So I hope you'll understand and forgive me.*

I think Luke realises what I'm going to do and why, and the fact that he has not tried to talk me out of it is the ultimate act of friendship. He's a wonderful man and I feel bad about the selfish way I've exploited our friendship in this way. I hope you can help him by offering him friendship and understanding. He's going to need both in the months ahead.

Jenna read no further as anger surged through her. *Selfish. Exploited our friendship.* The words leapt at her.

'Oh Luke,' she whispered into the gathering darkness, remembering his pain as he'd talked about John's death. 'How could he do that to you? And how could Mum spread all those lies? But, worst of all, how could *I*? Mum hated

269

you, rightly or wrongly, but I loved you. I still love you. How could I have said those dreadful things to you, believed you could do such a thing? How you must hate the whole damn Manning family!'

She dragged a sheaf of rainbow-coloured tissues from a box on her mother's dressing table, wiped her eyes and forced herself to read on.

I'm not afraid of death and I've had a great life, her father went on. I'm sorry things didn't work out between your mother and me, but we married too young. Our marriage never stood a chance. I think maybe climbers shouldn't marry. We're a selfish lot and once bitten with the climbing bug . . . Your poor mother thought if I loved her, I'd stop. But how could I? It was like asking me to stop breathing. I couldn't do it. I regret it now, though. Perhaps if I'd tried harder, who knows?

The thing I regret most is that I

won't be around to see you and James grow up. And of course I regret promising your mother not to take you climbing until you were old enough to decide for yourself about the risks. She was frightened I'd turn you into another climber. Oh, my dear, how I wish I had. How I wish that you were up here now with me and Luke.

Keeping that promise was the hardest thing I've ever done — except for watching your mother drive away from Brackwith with you and James in the back. Remember saying your goodbyes to the chickens and sheep? Well, I hope, in fact, I've made sure you'll go back to Brackwith soon and that when you do you'll help Luke shake off this terrible burden I've placed on him.

It's wonderful here, high above the snowline where eagles soar in a sky so blue it hurts your eyes to look at it. It's a magical place to spend my last days on this earth and I could never repay the debt I owe Luke in getting me here.

You probably know by now that I've left Brackwith to both you and Luke, in the hope that the two of you will become friends. Brackwith is a special place for me — for you, too, I hope. Some of my most precious memories are of us up on Bob's Crag and Brackwith Pike. Remember? You were a natural climber. James never shared your passion for Brackwith, so I've left him the royalties on my two best-selling books instead. I hope you don't mind. It probably means he's got the better deal financially, but I think, I hope, Brackwith means more than money to you.

I've written to James, but I've let him believe my death is an accident. But I feel — I know — that you are strong enough to hear the truth.

I must stop writing now. I am running out of paper . . . and time . . . but I don't know how to. How do I say a last goodbye to somebody I *love as much as I love you?*

Take care of yourself, Jenna. Have a happy life. Remember that poem you used to recite when you were little? The one about climbing above the shadow of the high mountain? Well, there are no shadows up here, my dearest daughter, only glorious sunshine.

I love you. I have loved you from the moment I saw you take your first breath. I shall go on loving you until the day I die — and forever beyond that.

God bless you, my dearest. Dad.

From the village came sounds of car doors closing, engines revving and driving off as churchgoers headed for home and Sunday evening television. Jenna, however, heard none of this. She strained against the dying light, reading and re-reading her father's letter, her emotions see-sawing between love for him, pity for herself, anger towards him, anger towards herself — then back again to love for him.

Her mother had been right about one thing. He had been an incredibly selfish man. How could he take himself off to die without giving her the chance to put things right between them?

And as for what he'd done to Luke . . . who was she kidding? Whatever her parents had done to Luke was as nothing compared with what she'd done to him. She tortured herself over and over with the words he'd flung after her as she'd run away from him in the hospital . . . *Your father died doing what he loved most in the world. I have to die little by little, trapped inside a body that soon won't get me up a flight of stairs, least of all a mountain.*

She stood up. Whatever she felt about her father, her mother, even Luke, was irrelevant. All that mattered was that Luke had been done a terrible wrong and she had to try to put things right.

She was halfway down the stairs when the doorbell rang. Grumbling inwardly at the possibility of delay, she flung open the door, determined to get rid of the caller quickly.

It was Julia Grantley.

'Jenna? It is Jenna, isn't it?' Her voice was low-pitched, her smile warm. 'I'm so glad I've found you. I was beginning to doubt Steven's directions as your lane seemed to go on for ever. I should have had more faith in him.'

'I'm sorry,' Jenna mumbled. 'This isn't a good time. I'm just on my way out and — '

She moved to step forward, to close the front door behind her as she did so, but Julia held her ground.

'Can I come in, Jenna, please?' she asked. She smiled again, and Jenna had to remind herself that this woman, too, had hurt Luke. *We have something in common after all*, she thought, with bitter irony.

'I'm sorry, but I'm in a dreadful hurry. As you can see, I really am on my way out.' Jenna indicated her coat and bag flung across her arm.

'This won't take long,' Julia persisted.

'But it is important. It's about Luke.'

'Luke?' Jenna was alarmed by Julia's grave expression. 'Is he all right?'

'Yes and no.' Julia followed Jenna into the kitchen, which bore the signs of Jenna's hasty attempted departure. She sat at the kitchen table and motioned Jenna to take the seat opposite. Jenna did so, picked up a teaspoon that had been left on the table and began twisting it between her fingers.

'Jenna, I don't know how much Luke has told you about him and me — '

'Look, Mrs Grantley — ' Jenna was determined to keep things between her and Julia as formal as possible. 'What goes on between you and Luke is nothing to do with me. And as for telling Luke about the man I saw you lunching with yesterday, I'm sorry. Sorry I upset Luke, that is. I don't want to know about your problems, Mrs Grantley, though — '

Julia looked blank, then, to Jenna's astonishment began to laugh. 'Jenna, that man you saw me with is my fiancé.'

'You're going to marry him? Does Luke know?'

'He was the first to know and is delighted. I'm sorry, I shouldn't tease you. You really don't know, do you? My dear, Luke and I aren't husband and wife. We're brother and sister.'

The teaspoon flipped from Jenna's fingers, soared into the air then landed with a clatter on the kitchen floor. But Jenna hadn't noticed. She stared at Julia, trying to take it in. Luke wasn't married to Julia . . . or anyone.

'You look shocked.' Julia retrieved the teaspoon. 'Whatever made you think I was his wife?'

'But he told me — ' Jenna stopped and forced herself to think back, to identify an occasion when he'd actually said that Julia was his wife. 'Sister Martin . . . he told Sister Martin . . . '

Julia laughed, crinkling her eyes and throwing her head back in the same way as Luke did. 'Apparently, he told Sister Martin he had a wife waiting for him at Brackwith, ready to give him round-the-clock tender loving care, as it was the only way he could get released from Colditz — his words, not mine. Then you turned up out of the blizzard and Sister M assumed you were the sainted Mrs Grantley and you went along with it, thereby earning Luke's undying gratitude.' She paused and looked closely at Jenna. 'Has he told you about our background?'

'A little. He said you went through a series of unsuitable foster homes.'

'Luke was the only stable thing in my childhood — mother, father, older brother and agony aunt all rolled into one. He was the one I turned to, even when — or rather, especially when — I was a spotty-faced teenager with boyfriend trouble.'

A picture of Luke flashed into Jenna's mind as Julia was speaking. He'd been telling her about his feelings for her father, describing him as the father he'd never had. Once again, she was ashamed of the jealousy — *he was the father I never had, as well!* — that had filled her at the time.

'Luke was determined that wherever he went, I went,' Julia was saying, 'And woe betide anyone who tried to split us up. He was a force to be reckoned with, even then.'

'I can imagine. No wonder you were so close.'

'Believe me, Jenna.' Julia's voice was low but emphatic. 'We're so close that when I hurt, he hurts and when he hurts, I hurt. And he's hurting now, I know it. That's why I'm here. From the little I've got out of Luke, he thinks you're with someone called Steven?'

'It's not as simple as that, I'm afraid. I only wish it was.'

'You mean you and this Steven — ?'

'Oh, heavens, no. It's — it's worse than that. I've done something unforgivable.'

'Do you want to tell me?'

'When I saw Luke yesterday, he looked very down,' Jenna said. 'He told me he was due to go into hospital again, but that things were pretty bleak.

Was he right? Are things as bad as he said? Is there really no hope?'

Julia bit her bottom lip. 'I don't know,' she said. 'I told you how I used to go to Luke with all my troubles and woes, but it doesn't work the other way round, I'm afraid. He never tells me a thing if he can help it but clams up. I'm a buyer for a fashion chain and I didn't even know about his accident until I got back to the UK from my latest trip. Because he knows that if I'd heard about it, I'd have dropped everything and come home.'

'His own worst enemy, according to Sister Martin.'

'She's not wrong. He's been in agony, both mental and physical, since his accident but he won't talk about it. I'm worried sick about him. He's always been such a fighter but now — well, it's as if he's given up.'

Jenna buried her face in her hands. An image of Luke's anguished face came to taunt her once more.

*Your father was the lucky one . . . I
have to die little by little in a useless
body that soon won't even get me up a
flight of stairs.*

'Jenna? Are you all right?' Julia laid a
comforting hand upon her shoulder.

'Please, Julia, don't be kind to me.'
Jenna looked up, tears trickling down
her face. 'You'll hate me when you
know what my family — what I have
done to him.'

'I won't hate you,' Julia said. 'And
I'm sure Luke doesn't.'

Jenna felt her father's letter crackle in
her pocket.

'And I'm sure he does,' she said.

'Surely — ' Julia began, but Jenna
forestalled her.

'I think I know what's upset Luke,'
she said, her voice little more than a
croak. 'Luke has been done a dreadful
wrong — by me, by my mother and by
my father, too.'

'John? Surely not!' Julia protested. 'I
can't . . . I won't believe it. He was so
good to Luke, so good to both of us, in

fact. He wouldn't do anything to hurt either of us.'

'No? Then why did he do this? He asked Luke to help him up a mountain, knowing he wouldn't be coming back down again alive. And, at the very end, he deliberately hid himself from Luke and the rescue party, so that he wouldn't be found until it was too late. He wanted to die up there and he tricked Luke into helping him do it.'

'But Luke wasn't responsible for John's death. The enquiry exonerated him.'

'But *I* didn't,' Jenna said with quiet emphasis. 'And my mother didn't — and neither, I think, did Luke himself. And that's the worst thing.'

Julia's eyes hardened. 'I'll never forget the day of John's funeral,' she said. 'He was in a terrible state. Your mother had told him to stay away so I didn't go either. He went climbing instead. On his own, the way he always does when he's got something on his mind. Only that time was different. I was so worried about him, and was about to call Mountain Rescue when he came back.'

Jenna felt a terrible chill, as if she was up on that cold mountain top. The numbness crept through her body, from her toes to the top of her head.

'Jenna, what is it?' Julia reached across and covered her hands as if to warm them. 'Tell me what's the matter. You've gone a terrible colour.'

Jenna looked up, then turned her face away. How could she tell her? How could she tell her what she'd done and watch her concern be replaced by hatred?

'It's my fault, Julia!' she cried. 'Luke's accident is my fault. He rang me after my mother died and I told him that I didn't want him to come to the funeral.'

'But I don't — '

'My mother's funeral was the day of his accident.' Jenna had to make Julia understand. 'If I hadn't told him to stay away — and remember, I was the second member of the Manning family to say that to him — he wouldn't have been out on Brackwith Pike that day.'

Julia took her hands away from Jenna's and stood up. She moved across to the kitchen window and stared out into the nothingness of a countryside night.

'My mother used to say there was no such thing as a climbing accident, there was always somebody at fault. Well, she was wrong about most things, but she was right about that.' Jenna gave a bitter, self-mocking laugh. 'My father's so-called accident was no accident. And as for Luke's — well, that's all down to me, I'm afraid.'

'I'm sure Luke doesn't see it that way,' Julia said without turning around.

'But even that isn't the worst thing.' Jenna took a deep breath, praying that Julia wouldn't turn around. What she had to say was easier to say to the back of her head than her face. 'Luke blamed himself — quite wrongly — for Dad's death and has lived with that guilt ever since. I — I fell in love with your brother, Julia and yet, I too blamed him. I said some dreadful things to him, things that can never be unsaid. What sort of love is that?'

Still Julia said nothing, but she turned around to face Jenna.

'I'm not trying to make excuses for what I said.' Jenna forced herself to meet Julia's steady gaze. 'I should have known he was incapable of the dreadful things I accused him of. I should have had more faith in him.

'But I didn't. Instead, at a time when he was at a low ebb, I made things a million times worse. My only excuse is that what I said to him was what I'd been brought up to believe was the truth. I know differently now, of course.'

With trembling hands, she took her father's final letter out of her coat pocket and handed it across the table to Julia.

'I think you have the right to read this, Julia,' she said heavily. 'And, when you have done, you should take it to Luke. He needs to know this, and I think it would be better coming from you. Because I'm quite sure that he won't ever want to see me again.'

17

After reading it a second time, Julia placed the letter on the table, taking care to put it back into its original folds. She cleared her throat.

'You know,' she said, concentrating on smoothing out imaginary creases, 'you and I have a lot in common. Probably more than you realise.'

'How do you mean?' Whatever Jenna had expected her to say, it was not this.

'I don't mean Luke, although there's him too, of course. I mean we've both been badly treated by our parents, but I had Luke to look out for me, while you had no one.'

'Oh, no,' Jenna protested. 'I can't hide the wrong I've done Luke behind some imaginary hurt done to me — '

'Imaginary hurt? Luke told me a bit about your mother — and now this . . . ' Julia tapped John's letter.

'How old were you when John wrote this? I was nineteen when he died and you must be a couple of years younger than me, so you'd have been . . . sixteen? Seventeen?'

'Seventeen. But I don't see — '

'Don't you? That letter's pretty hard to deal, isn't it? How do you think you'd have felt if you'd read it at the time of his death, when you were still little more than a child?'

'At least I'd have known he still loved me.'

'You must have known that anyway. John adored you. He was always talking about you. How could you not know?'

'It's complicated and all my fault. He tried many times to make things right between us but I wouldn't let him. Ask Luke. He'll tell you.'

'There's more than one way to ill-treat children, you know, and I stick by what I said. We have more in common that you realise. Here.' She handed Jenna the letter. 'You should take this to Luke yourself.'

'I can't. Things have gone too wrong between us. Seeing me will only make things worse for him and I've done him enough harm already.'

Julia placed both hands gently on Jenna's shoulders and looked into her eyes. 'I thought you said you loved him,' she said softly. 'You do, don't you?'

Jenna nodded.

'Then prove it.' Julia's eyes bored into hers. 'Luke's in a bad way, that's why I'm here. I think this letter could help, but only if it helps the two of you sort out your problems. Otherwise it's an irrelevance. Don't you see that? It's in the past. Gone. Finished. What matters is you and Luke. He cares for you, Jenna. I know he does. He cares very deeply.'

Jenna frowned. Surely Julia had got it wrong. Or was she playing a cruel trick on her?

'After all I've said to him? After all my family has done to him? No — I just don't believe it. Has he ever said anything about it to you?'

'Lord, no,' Julia said, with a wry laugh. 'But that's Luke, isn't it? He always keeps his feelings to himself, except for yesterday when he thought you were living with Steven. Boy, was he mad! It's a good job that Steven wasn't around. I think he'd have torn him apart.'

'But . . . ' Jenna still didn't dare let herself hope it might be true. 'Why didn't he say? If it's true, why didn't he say something?'

'Oh that's easy. My stupid brother likes making other people's decisions for them and he's decided it's not fair to saddle you with someone in his condition.'

'He told you this?' Jenna said, stunned. 'How dare he discuss that with anyone, before talking to me!'

'Of course he didn't. I've already said, he never talks about his problems to anyone. But I know him, I know him better than he knows himself.'

'I'm afraid you've misread the signs.' Jenna's throat tightened with disappointment. She swallowed hard, blinked and forced a smile. 'I'm sorry, I'm quite sure it will do him more harm than good to see me. Every time we meet, we end up hurting each other, so it's best we stay apart, for now, at least. Maybe later on, if he wants to see me, well, who knows?'

Julia uttered a short, sharp swear word. 'Sorry,' she said. 'But I hate it when he's right and I'm wrong. I was so sure . . .'

'Right about what?'

'Why, you, of course. He said it would be wrong to ask you to commit yourself to him in his condition, that you wouldn't want to know. Maybe, just maybe, the operation will work. Then, as you've just said, who knows?'

Jenna was furious and disappointed that just as she was beginning to like Julia, she'd got something so wrong.

'How dare you make presumptions about my feelings for Luke! My love for him isn't conditional on whether or not he walks again.'

'Then prove it.' Julia turned on her

like a cat about to pounce. 'If you love my brother as you say you do, prove it by letting him see that, whatever the outcome of the operation, it won't make any difference to your feelings for him.'

'But he won't — '

'Please, give him something to fight for.' Julia blinked back tears as she took Jenna's hand. 'He's giving up, and it terrifies me to see him like that. I'm sorry I was so horrible to you just now. I only said it to provoke a reaction. And it was the right one. I knew I couldn't be that wrong about you.

'He's having his operation tomorrow morning and they say you can visit any time after six pm. Please say you'll go.'

Jenna drew a deep breath. 'You don't know what you're asking, Julia. But yes, I will — I owe him that.'

'And you'll give him the letter?'

'You don't give up, do you?' Jenna managed a weak smile. 'Okay, I'll give him the letter.'

'I never give up.' Julia chuckled.

'Now, were you making some coffee or — ?' She stopped in mid-sentence, her hand to her mouth. 'No — I remember now — you were on your way out when I frog-marched you in here. I'm so sorry. I hope I haven't upset your plans.'

'You won't believe this — ' Jenna grinned ruefully — 'but I was about to set off for London to see Luke. Stupid of me, because it would be too late to see him by the time I got there. Besides — and I promise this has only just occurred to me — I don't even know which hospital he's in, which goes to show what my state of mind is. So, in fact, it's just as well that you turned up when you did.'

★ ★ ★

It was early afternoon when Jenna got back to Sarah's house. One part of her was thankful that Sarah was at work, as it would spare her the inevitable questions, but the rest would have welcomed any distraction, even difficult questions, from the agony of worrying about Luke and watching the clock creep towards six o'clock, the time she was longing for and dreading in equal measure.

She got to the hospital a little after six, half-hoping Julia had got it wrong and that Luke was not allowed visitors that evening. But the receptionist smiled and said that of course she could see him, and gave directions to his room.

She opened the door quietly, thinking of the disastrous way her last hospital visit had ended. Luke was lying back against the pillows, their whiteness accentuating the pallor of his skin. He looked so vulnerable that Jenna had to stop herself leaning across and kissing those lips that looked as if they had been recently bitten against the pain. But although she resisted the tempta-tion to kiss him, she reached out her hand and, with a gentle finger, pushed the hair that had fallen over his face back in place. As she did so, his eyes opened. Her heart did a somersault at the warmth of his smile.

'The same healing hands, I see,' he murmured. 'Just what the doctor ordered.'

'So how are you feeling?' she whispered, more because of the tightness of her throat than any desire to be quiet.

'I'm fine,' he said. 'How are you?'

She shrugged and pushed her fingers through her damp hair. 'Oh, I'm fine, too,' she said. 'But wet. It's pouring with rain out there. You're in the best place, you know.'

As if from a distance, she heard her own voice, prattling on, aware of how unnatural she sounded. *Julia, I'm sorry, she cried inwardly, you're going to hate me. But I can't sit here, making small-talk one minute and, the next, drop into the conversation the fact that I love him. I'm a coward and every other insult you can think of . . . but I can't do it.*

'Are you sure you're all right?' he asked.

Jenna forced a laugh. 'Hey, that's my line. I'm the one who's supposed to be asking you that. I'm tired, that's all.'

'Oh? Any particular reason?'

'I've been at the cottage this weekend, clearing out. And I — I had a visitor.'

Luke glared. 'Steven?' It was more a snarl than a question.

'No, not Steven.' Was Julia right after all? Could it be that Luke really was jealous of him?

'Steven, as far as I know, spent a blissful Sunday with my housemate, Sarah. The two of them have been an item for some time now.'

He held her gaze. 'So, who was your visitor if it wasn't Steven, then?'

'My visitor?' Jenna took a deep breath and willed her voice to sound normal. 'It was Julia. And, Luke, I made the silliest mistake. I thought she was your wife, not your sister.'

'I know you did.' He eased himself

into a more comfortable position. 'The last time we met, you accused me of using you to get back at her for her unfaithfulness.'

'That wasn't all my fault,' she protested. 'You deceived me when we first met — or rather, I jumped to the wrong conclusion and you made no attempt to put me right.'

'Well, that makes us even in the deception stakes, Jane Bennington, doesn't it?' he said. 'And I tried to tell you in the park, but you stormed off before I could do so.'

She flushed. 'I know. I was stupid. I'm sorry, Luke. I made a complete idiot of myself. I — I guess I was jealous.'

'Jealous?' His left eyebrow arched in that familiar gesture that made Jenna's heart skip a beat every time he did it. 'Why?'

'Because I — '

Now! the voice inside screamed. *Finish the sentence. Tell him it was because you love him. Do it now!*

But she couldn't. As she leaned forward, she felt the presence of her father's letter in her handbag, pressing into her lap as if it had suddenly expanded to ten times its original weight. It would be an act of selfishness to think of her own feelings for Luke until her father's letter was out in the open and she'd made some attempt to put things right. No more hiding. Luke had a right to the truth.

'I found this letter addressed to me in my mother's desk. I'd like you to read it.'

He took the letter and frowned as he recognised the handwriting. 'It's from John.'

Jenna nodded. 'It's a letter he wrote to me on his last trip,' she said. 'Please read it and, as you do, try to forgive me.'

She watched his face intently as he read the letter. She saw the pain and sorrow she'd expected to see but there was something else, another emotion she couldn't identify.

When at last he spoke, it was in such a low voice she had to lean towards him to hear.

'I knew what he intended to do,' he said. 'Or, at least, I had a pretty good idea and at first the only thing I felt, apart from grief, of course, was pride. I was proud he'd chosen me. I thought it proved that the love I felt for him was not one-sided, that he must have loved and trusted me to want me with him at such a time.'

'He did love you, Luke. I know he did.' She leaned across and took his hand. 'And if I live to be one hundred and ten, that won't be enough time to make up for all the terrible things I and my family, including Dad, have done to you. It's no excuse to say I didn't know, that I've only just found out. I should have trusted you. I should have known — '

Luke put a finger on her lips. 'Let me finish, Jenna. Please. It's important.'

Her lips were burning under the gentle pressure of his fingers and she

299

longed to part her lips slightly and kiss them. But she held back.

'As I said,' he went on, 'I'd a good idea what he planned to do. And that was why I felt guilty. Not for failing to find him in time; there was no way anyone would have found John if he didn't want to be found. But I should have persuaded him to talk the whole thing through — maybe persuaded him to get a second opinion, more tests, who knows? I felt I should've tried that, but I didn't. That's what I felt guilty about.'

'You haven't carried that guilt all this time, have you?'

Luke shook his head. 'I'm afraid not. Your mother did me a favour, albeit unwittingly. She gave me such a hard time that I'd painted this grotesque picture of you all as a bunch of money-grabbers to whom John owed nothing. It wasn't until I met you that I realised how badly you'd been treated, not only by her, but by him, too. It was selfish of him not to have put things right between you and him before he died.

'And it was painful to find, after all these years, that my hero had feet of clay. That was when I began to feel guilty about not doing more to talk him out of his plans. So guilty, in fact, that when you accused me of causing his death, I agreed with you. I should have done my best to stop him.'

Jenna leaned across the bed and kissed him full on the lips, the way she'd been longing to do the moment she'd first entered the room. She pulled back and looked down at him, her eyes glowing with love and shining with tears.

'I don't know about you,' she whispered, 'but I think I prefer my heroes to have feet of clay. It makes them more human, don't you think? I think, too, that it's time to put the past where it belongs, in the past, and concentrate on the future.'

'And do we have a future?' Luke's eyes searched her face.

'I'm beginning to think we might.' She leaned forward to kiss him again with all the glorious confidence of a woman who loves and who knows — or at least, is pretty sure — that she is loved in return.

'That is . . . ' she kissed the fan of lines around his eyes, ' . . . I sincerely hope so because I . . . ' she broke off to kiss the scar on his cheekbone, ' . . . I love you, Luke,' she whispered, her voice dying away as their lips met in a kiss that sent bubbles of happiness fizzing through her veins once more.

Then Luke winced and pulled back. 'This isn't good for a man in my position.'

Jenna gave a cry of dismay. 'Oh, what a fool. What a stupid, clumsy fool I've been. If I've done you any damage, I'll never forgive myself — '

'That, too, belongs in the past, Jenna,' Luke said firmly. 'I can't bear to hear you talk that way about yourself. Of course you haven't done me any damage. In fact, you have just done me more good than all the doctors in the world.'

'Nevertheless — ' She stood up and headed for the door, all her earlier confidence evaporating. 'I shouldn't have said . . . or done . . . Forget it. You're looking tired. I'll go now and leave you to get some rest.'

'Jenna!' he called. 'Please come back. I have something to tell you. Something important. Sit down . . . please.'

She perched unwillingly on the edge of the chair.

'I want to say that I love you,' he said, speaking slowly and carefully, as if it was a speech he'd rehearsed carefully. 'I think I've loved you all my life, in a way. I loved you when you came crashing into my bedroom, looking as if you'd seen a ghost; I loved you when you played the clarinet with the tears streaming down your face; I loved you when you showed me a neat way with spreadsheets and I loved you when you protected me from Sister Martin, who frightens the life out of me.'

As he spoke, Jenna watched for signs that he was teasing, scarcely daring to breathe in case she should break the spell. She longed to throw herself into his arms, to kiss him, to hold him, to have him repeat over and over again those wonderful, magical words that she'd thought she would never hear. He loved her! He really, truly loved her. She felt the colour stain her cheeks and, as she often did at moments of heightened emotion, said the first thing that came in to her head.

'Terrified of Sister Martin? I can't imagine you terrified of anyone or anything.'

'Oh, but I am,' he said. 'I'm terrified of losing you, my love.'

She caught her breath. 'That you'll never do,' she whispered. 'You're stuck with me now for the rest of your life.'

'Is that a promise?'

She nodded, smiling. 'It's a promise. But why didn't you tell me sooner? You must have known how I felt about you. I was never any good at hiding my feelings and gave myself away several times. In fact, once I thought I'd actually spoken out loud but when you didn't react, I realised I'd — '

'You did speak out loud.'

'Then why — ? If you knew you loved me, back then, why didn't you say anything?'

'Because — ' He hesitated and shifted, wincing as he did so. 'Because I didn't think it was fair to saddle you with a man who can't walk.'

How well Julia knew this adorable, infuriating, incredibly maddening brother of hers! 'But whether or not you can walk makes no difference at all to me. Surely you know that?'

'No, I didn't think it would to you,' he said. 'But it sure makes a difference to me.'

'Of course,' she said. 'I can understand that. But what's made you change your mind about telling me now?'

'What made me change my mind about telling you I love you and want to marry you?' Luke's face had the look of a child who'll burst if he doesn't share his secret with somebody. 'This place. They think I'm some sort of medical miracle.'

'You mean — ' Jenna hardly dared voice her hope, in case she was wrong.

'Apparently everything's going back together far better than anyone dared hope and although it's early days and they're being cautious, they're now being cautiously optimistic. This morning's operation went like a dream, I'm told. So they're now saying that, with the help of enough judiciously placed bits of hardware — which was what this morning's operation was all about — and provided I'm a good boy, eat up my greens and do my exercises, there's every chance that I'll regain full mobility in both legs.'

'Luke! That's the best — does Julia know?' Her words tumbled over themselves in her excitement. 'I'm so happy for you — for us — so very happy,' she said and burst into tears.

He held out his arms to her and she

went into them gladly, but cautiously, afraid of hurting him again. But he pulled her closer and she relaxed into the delicious sensation of crying on his shoulder. She thought of the last time she'd done so in the Barn at Brackwith. Then, they'd been tears of unexpressed sadness. Now they were tears of relief and joy.

'Think of it, my love,' he said, his breath fanning her hair. 'Think of all the things I'll be able to do that I didn't dare think about this time last week; this time yesterday, even. I'll be able to walk down the aisle with you on our wedding day. Then there's Brackwith . . . ' He held her away from him at arms' length, the happiness in his eyes chasing away all the dark shadows that had lurked there for so long. 'The dreams I had to put on hold after my accident have all become possible. I'll be the one to teach the kids to climb and abseil — '

Momentarily she froze, then pulled away from him, her heart thudding.

'Climb? You're going to teach them to climb? But how? I mean — '

He was so caught up in his vision that he failed to notice her voice had hardened.

'I know,' he said happily. 'It's unbelievable, isn't it? But the consultant said that, if I'm careful, there's no reason why I shouldn't manage a little gentle rock climbing, although he thought it might be better to leave the Himalayas until this time next year.'

Jenna felt as if her blood had turned to ice and there was a full-scale avalanche pounding inside her head. She freed her hands and stepped away from the bed.

'The Himalayas?' she echoed. 'Are you telling me you intend to climb again?'

'Maybe not the Himalayas. Not yet,' he said, and Jenna fancied she could already see that look in his eyes — the same faraway look her father used to get.

'But clearly you do intend to go on

climbing as soon as you're fit enough?'

The light died in his eyes. 'I'm a climber, Jenna,' he said in a slow, careful voice. 'It's what I do. You knew that all along.'

'But I didn't — ' she began, but stopped. What was the point? She turned away from him and stared out of the window where street lights gleamed dull through the haze of rain.

'Do you want me to give up climbing?' he asked, still in that same controlled voice.

'Would you?' She whirled round. But hope died within her as she saw him hesitate — and she knew that, once again, she had lost out to the mountains.

If he loved her, really loved her, he wouldn't have to stop and think about it. He wouldn't have hesitated like that.

'It's no good, Luke,' she whispered, her voice close to breaking. 'You and me — it's no good. It won't work. I'm my mother's daughter, you see. I have the same fears, the same loathing, if you like, of climbing.'

She choked back a sob and went on, 'I love you too much to ask you to give it up. It's part of who you are, as you say. I spent a large part of my early childhood watching my parents tear each other apart over the same thing. They made each other's lives, and those around them, a misery and I can't do that, Luke. I can't live the sort of life she did. I can't marry you.'

18

This final insurmountable barrier to their happiness together had arisen so suddenly, so unexpectedly, that it had taken them both by surprise.

A couple of times, Luke drew breath as if he was about to say something, but each time thought better of it. Eventually, it was Jenna who broke the silence.

'I'm sorry,' she murmured. 'So very sorry. I've hurt you, yet again, but surely you can see . . . '

'Oh, I see, all right,' he cut in, his voice bitter. 'What I see is someone who thought she loved me when she believed I was disabled, an object of pity. But as for taking on the whole man, that's too much reality for you, lady, isn't it? You carry on hiding behind your mother's fears and prejudices. You say you don't want to live the kind of life she lived, but can't you see you're already doing just that?'

His eyes challenged her. She said nothing, but stared down at her feet as his angry words washed over her.

'Fine,' he spat. 'That's fine. You carry on holding those apron strings because obviously you're not ready to let go yet. Let me know when you finally grow up, Jenna. I might, just might, still be around, but I can't guarantee it. When I leave here, I'll be going straight back to Brackwith. If you want me, you'll have to come there to find me — because I won't come after you.'

* * *

Jenna could remember little of leaving the hospital that night, apart from being thankful for the rain lashing into her face, disguising her tears. She was thankful, too, that Sarah was out when she finally got back. She didn't want to have to explain her swollen eyes to anyone, least of all someone as sympathetic as Sarah. She grabbed some more clothes and books, left yet another note for Sarah and fled back to Somerset.

It was after midnight when she reached Chedcombe. She let herself in, not minding the bleakness of the near-empty cottage, for that was how she felt inside — bleak and empty.

For the rest of the week she went through the motions of living. Looking back on it later, she had no recollection of how she'd filled her time. She supposed she must have done ordinary, everyday things like getting up, shopping, preparing meals, but had only a vague impression of moving like a sleepwalker through the fog of her misery.

At some time Mr Bennington phoned to tell her completion on the cottage had been put back a fortnight, giving her a little more time. Even so, she left the final clearing-out of her mother's desk, which she'd abandoned the night Julia arrived, until the rest of the cottage had all been packed up, the furniture either sent into storage or sold and awaiting collection. Only the desk remained and that, she realised, she could put off no longer.

The top three drawers, one of which had contained her father's letter, had already been dealt with. The fourth drawer contained school reports and photographs of herself and James. The sight of her thin, freckled face scowling out of almost every photograph caused her to smile for the first time in almost two long weeks.

In the bottom drawer, the last, was a cardboard box containing letters, pictures and cuttings, all of her father, and, tucked away in the bottom right-hand corner, two silver horseshoes carefully wrapped in tissue paper. From her parents' wedding cake? Why had her mother kept these things? Most divorcees wipe out all trace of their former partners. Why, the only thing missing was a blue ribbon, then the box would be like a collection of lovers' keepsakes.

She looked down at her right hand where she still wore her mother's wedding ring.

'Oh, Mum,' she whispered, as she took off the ring, wrapped it in the tissue paper with the horseshoes and placed it in the box. 'You never stopped loving him, did you? Yet you went through all the pain of divorce. How could you have given up on your love? You could have sorted things out, if you'd both tried.'

It was as if the sun had come out after weeks of unrelenting rain. Was she going to end up like her mother, with nothing more to show for her love than one sad little box of pictures and press cuttings? No way!

She rushed through the few jobs still to be done at the cottage, threw the last of her personal things into the car and began the long drive north, stopping only to drop in the key to Edward

Bennington and, briefly later, for petrol and a hastily-eaten sandwich.

* * *

It was late afternoon when she turned up the track to Brackwith. She had to force herself to take the rough, stony track at a steady pace. She pulled into the yard, jumped out and almost ran into the house in her impatience to see Luke.

He wasn't there. She looked in the kitchen, where the cat blinked a sort of welcome. She looked in the study and the small bedroom off it. Finally, she ran up the stairs, calling his name, looking in every room. But he wasn't in any of them.

And yet he was staying here. Julia had told her Luke had been discharged and had gone back to Brackwith over a week ago now. Besides, his books, clothes, even his boots, were scattered about the place.

She went from one empty room to

another, and the elation that had carried her from Somerset to Brackwith burst like a child's balloon. He could be anywhere. Out with friends. Or back in hospital. Had something gone wrong? Had some of the 'hardware' that he'd joked about malfunctioned? *Not that. Please don't let it be that.*

She paced about the empty house until, unable to bear the silence any longer, she went outside. Slumping down on the doorstep, she looked up as a buzzard wheeled overhead, making its plaintive mewling sound as other birds chased it away from their nesting sites.

As she watched, her eyes were drawn to a patch of colour up on Bob's Crag. Something, or someone, was up there.

It was Luke. She recognised him even from this distance, but confirmed it when she fetched her binoculars from the car. How had he got that far? And how was he going to get down? With a jolt of fear, she realised he hadn't moved.

She grabbed her walking boots,

which were better than the slip-on shoes she was wearing, and raced towards the foot of the crag.

'Luke?' Her voice bounced off the rough grey rock. 'Are you all right?'

After an agonisingly long time, she caught his reply. 'I'm stuck. Help me.'

She looked up at the cliff-face above her and took a deep breath. Could she remember the route her father had taught her? It had been many years. Was it like riding a bike? Would it all come back to her?

'Please, Dad,' she whispered. 'You helped me do this before. Help me now.'

She began her ascent, her confidence returning with every step, every remembered move. She hesitated several times, and as she did so heard her father's voice, felt his presence by her side. 'Reach for it, Jenna,' he urged. 'Go on. You're doing absolutely fine.'

And she was. By the time she neared Luke's ledge, she was moving as easily and freely across the rock as she'd done when her father had climbed with her. In spite of her anxiety, she realised she still enjoyed the exhilaration of finding the right handhold in the right place; the rock warm beneath her hands; the whip of the wind as it ruffled her hair.

'Luke. Are you . . . ?' she began as she reached his ledge, where he sat, as relaxed as if he'd been waiting for her under the railway station clock.

'What took you so long?' He grinned.

Things she could have said to him, about frightening her, being irresponsible, putting them both in danger, flashed into her head. But she said none of them. Instead, she sat down beside him.

'I grew up,' she said. 'You told me to come back when I had, so here I am. Are you still around?'

He looked down at the narrow ledge, then up at the rockface stretching high above them. 'I'm not going anywhere,' he said.

'How did you get up here?'

'The same way as you did, my love.

Slowly and carefully at first, then more confident with every step. It seems John taught us both well.'

She nodded. 'So, the next question has to be — how are we going to get you down?'

'Who said anything about going down?'

'But you said you were — ' She broke off and glared at him. 'You're not stuck at all, are you?'

He shook his head. 'Would you have come up otherwise?'

'Well . . . no, probably not. But you were taking a huge chance. What if I'd slipped or got stuck?'

'Not you.' He smiled. 'You're a natural. John always said you were, and watching you just now, I can see he was right. You kept telling me you're your mother's daughter. Well, I felt it was time to remind you that you're your father's daughter too.'

'You mean, you *planned* this? But how?'

'I've been climbing Bob's Crag every day for weeks even before I went to

London — sometimes with sticks, sometimes without, to build up my strength. I promised myself that when you came, as I knew you would sooner or later, somehow I'd get you to come up here. When I heard your car coming along the track I was already part way up here and knew it was too good a chance to waste. So I got to the ledge and waited — and here you are.'

'Here I am.' She shuffled along the ledge. 'Luke, I've done a lot of — '

'Jenna, I must — '

They laughed as they both started to speak at the same time. Jenna gestured to Luke to carry on.

'The things I said, about not giving up climbing for you,' he said. 'I've thought about little else for the last couple of weeks, except how meaningless life is without you. I judged you too harshly, not taking into account your upbringing. That was selfish of me. Darling Jenna, you're more important to me than anything in my life, and that includes climbing. And if that's what it takes to keep you, I promise I'll never climb again.'

'You'd do that for me?' Her voice sounded incredulous.

This time there was no hesitation. 'If that's what it takes, I'll do it gladly.'

'Luke, you don't know what it means to hear you say that,' she said. 'But you don't have to. I came up here to tell you that my love for you isn't conditional. You're a climber, hence you climb — and I'll never ask you to stop doing so.'

'Do you mean that?' He drew a sharp breath as he looked at her. The wind had whipped colour into her cheeks and her eyes shone with happiness.

She nodded. 'However, coming up here today has changed some things.'

'It has?' He looked anxious.

'I think that maybe, now and again, I might come with you — if you'll have me.' She laughed as she saw his look of delight.

'There's one thing, though.' She was serious again. 'One day, I'd like you to take me to where Dad died. I have some things of Mum's I'd like to leave there. Would you — or would it be too painful for you?'

He raised her hand and kissed her fingers. 'My darling, I'd love to. I think it will help us both lay John's ghost to rest. Now,' he rubbed her hands between his, 'it's getting chilly. Your hands are like ice. Shall we go down, or on up to the next ridge? There's — '

'A fantastic view from there.' She finished the sentence for him. 'I remember it and I'd love to see it again. Let's go.'

As they climbed together, a snatch of her father's letter ran through her head.

Remember the poem about the shadow of the high mountain? he'd written. *There are no shadows up here, my dearest daughter — only glorious sunshine.*

And together, Luke and Jenna climbed towards the sunshine.

AS TIME GOES BY

Gillian Villiers

When Lally caretakes her grand-mother's croft in the wildest part of Scotland, she fully expects that she'll return soon, to a high-powered job in Edinburgh. Her scatterbrained sister Bel has other plans though, and Lally quickly finds the people and the place seeping into her soul. Or is it just one person, in the shape of new neighbour Iain? Torn between two worlds, Lally's decision will not only impact on herself, but also on everyone else around her.

A CERTAIN SMILE

Beth James

Freya has been made redundant and her high-flying boyfriend, Jay, is pressurising her to join him in London. But this would mean her leaving the place her heart lies — her home in the New Forest. And there are so many things to consider: her friends, her small cottage and her adorable, little dog Henri . . . and there's a certain dog walker with good legs and a friendly smile. Freya knows that she'd miss saying 'good morning' to him too.

CORY'S GIRLS

Teresa Ashby

Mark Jacobs returns to his home town to settle old scores, but learns that his ex-wife died two years before. Emma, his daughter from that marriage, and with whom he'd lost contact, is settled and happy with Cory Elliot, her stepfather, and her two half-sisters. But Mark wants her back, and when Cory has to go abroad on business, he leaves the girls with Katrina, who has to fight to keep the family together for Cory — the man she loves.

WHERE LOVE BELONGS

Chrissie Loveday

Lizzie Vale, Nellie Cobridge's youngest sibling, has to make a decision. What will she do with her life? Journalism excites her, but in 1938 it's not easy for a woman to get a job in this field, however bright and lively she is. Determined to succeed, she tries various schemes and tackles everything with enthusiasm. Fortunately, she has the support of a loving family when things go wrong. She meets Charlie and her future seems set. Or is it?

DREAMS OF TOMORROW

Toni Anders

When artist Jessica Lawrence was jilted, just before her wedding, she determined to concentrate on her career and ignore men. However, at a party she meets contented bachelor Ian Grantly. There is a mutual attraction which they both fight against. Then, during holidays in Cornwall and Italy, the attraction grows. But whilst Jessica believes that he will never settle down, and Ian thinks that she may return to her fiancé, how can they ever find happiness together?

CHARLIE'S WAR

Linda Gruchy

Five years ago, Matt broke Charlie's heart and walked out of her life. Now, just as Charlie is about to marry Kent, Matt returns, oblivious to the hurt he caused her. Charlie knows she's doing the right thing in marrying Kent. But Kent has dark secrets that Charlie knows nothing about, secrets which only come to light when tragedy strikes . . .